ENCOUNTERING DARKNESS

Paul Brandt

ENCOUNTERING DARKNESS: The Great
Pursuit Series, Book 1

Copyright © 2017 Paul Brandt

Cover design: betibup33 design at https:// twitter.com/ BetiBup33

Editors: Johnathan and Sonya Martin

Acknowledgments

Thank you for taking the time to read Encountering Darkness. Without you, I wouldn't have an audience.

A special thanks to my editors, Johnathan and Sonya Martin, for their fresh eyes and advice in making this book. I appreciate the help!

To my friends and family, I would like to thank you for your support throughout my life.

Last, I thank God for giving me a passion and desire to create. While I write with the purpose of reaching people, I as well write for an audience of one and hope this book shares, even a little, of God's glory.

CHAPTER ONE

Pete was standing outside of his home, on his front porch. He was leaning on the white railing which went on along the deck. With a drink of jack and coke in hand, Pete looked around at all he had made in Winfield. He saw the new school and the hospital in the background; he made those because he was able to get the job completed. Pete increased the income of the police force and fireman and was also bearing down on getting teacher pay raised. He was admired by everybody and contributed to many charities, making certain that people would recognize his contributions.

Winfield, an insignificant town, sat in the center of no-man's-land. The climate was mild with only a less-than-average, but expected, rainfall. In spite of this, Winfield was lush with vegetation. The only area of concern was the grass. The town's grass was sporadically distributed throughout the town. Only one place had ample grass, but Pete was seeking to change that. Although, even in the one area, the grass was much poorer than one would expect in this region.

Because of this, few people had high hopes for this town of about 15,000, but this was changing. Along the stretch of the road before him, Pete gazed at the small shops which opened just a block down the street. A barber, salon, and a sushi establishment were its latest additions.

"It's strange, I mean today is strange," remarked Pete Pethaford out loud to himself.

Although Pete was observing the grand splendor, he thought today was strange because no one was out and there weren't even cars on the street. It looked as if everything in the town was desolate and nothing was going on. It moved him so much today that no one was out; he had to consider where everybody might be.

He recalled where everyone went to on this day and he pitied those people. Even as there was always an important message; something about hope and salvation…blah…blah…blah. He perceived they were only destroying themselves. The man in black had to give a message about end times, and how the end times are approaching just to get people to pay attention to him.

Pete chuckled at that conclusion and declared, once again to himself, "People are continually ranting about end times, but no one actually understands what they are saying." Pete was addressing one of his white posts, and with a large grin, he gave it a kick.

After a few minutes with the encounter with the post, he went back inside his house to wait for the people to come back. He went through to the kitchen but turned away after he noticed a foul stench.

"I guess I will clean that up later," he said to himself.

His kitchen often smelled awful, so he often needed to clean it. He walked to his family room so he could watch some TV, but turned away from that room after he observed it was a mess. This was a little more unusual since it was common for the rest of Pete's house to be in good order.

He left that room and instead went on to his bedroom to sleep. When he was ascending the stairs, he noticed the sunlight appeared to be brighter, but he shrugged that off and continued to his room to rest. While he was in his room, he observed the window was open and that it was cold so he closed it. When he went to the window he looked out and recognized the grass wasn't green anymore. He thought it was strange, but still went to his bed to sleep. It was 12 pm.

He slept for an extended period in peaceful bliss. When he woke up, he noticed the clock read 6 pm. He thought it was odd, but the air seemed mustier and something didn't seem right; something was unusual. He got up and glanced around his bedroom and everything seemed to be the same, but the air was different. If it was possible, the air smelled cleaner and fresher, but his room still carried a musty smell that obscured the clean air.

"Must be roaches," Pete said softly to himself.

He decided, after some thought, to leave his room and go back down stairs. As he descended the steps, he noticed that the sun wasn't out anymore, but rather the clouds veiled the sun. As he drew near to the bottom of the stairs, he recognized the horrid smell again, but this time it was so strong that it was burning his nose. He then sneezed once, sneezed once more, coughed, wheezed, and gagged his way down the rest of the flights of stairs, until he gave in, and let out things from his innards. After he reached the ground floor, he fell, and laid on the floor for minutes which appeared to go on forever. Pete was trembling as he was still coughing and throwing up. He then passed out.

When he woke up, he couldn't move, but rather laid there until he could will his body to move. He didn't dare breathe through his nose, but instead his breathing came from his mouth in rapid pants. After several moments of blundering, he got up, and ran to the front entrance. It was his escape! When he got to the door, because he was so out of it, he took awhile to open it.

After unlocking the door, in rushed the cool fresh air, and he stumbled outside to his freedom. He fell down to the earth and let it engulf him. Then he felt himself fade away and let himself completely go.

When he woke up, the sun was blazing and the birds went on singing, well … somewhat. The birds took the several hours he was unconscious to receive free food. They continued pecking at him the entire time he was passed out, but he was too much into his dreams to care. The birds forgot what was provision and what was a soul, so he had small pieces picked out of his body.

When he inspected himself he discovered that the birds had cleaned him and except for the holes in his body he felt good.

He got up and glanced around, and he could hear a bee in the distance, as if he was in a dream.

"Dream!" Pete yelled. "Maybe this was just a dream! Of course! Nothing like this takes place in real life," he reassured himself.

Pete, even in a dream, could understand he was dreaming. He had this happen ever since he was a child and researched what the phenomenon was called when he grew older. From what Pete could tell, through investigation, he had lucid dreams and night terrors. Although, he could perceive he was dreaming, he found that he couldn't shake himself up from one even if he desired to. Because of that recollection, Pete went back to his house, but stopped short at the door. He paused until he could be certain there would be nothing happening inside.

Unlike what is expected, he at once opened the door and drew a whiff of air when it was open. He coughed a little because of the musty air, but the other death smell was gone and he was glad.

Pete took a few more steps into the house and the musty odor was likewise gone. He used that instance to acknowledge himself for his courage, even if it was only a dream.

He was wondering if the other smell was gone in the kitchen, so he moved towards it. As he approached the kitchen, he noticed the scent was gone, but something just didn't seem normal, so he turned around just before drawing near to the entrance of the kitchen.

CHAPTER TWO

Throughout the week that followed, Pete enjoyed his time very much. People continued on walking about the streets, laughing and having fun. Pete was glad for the difference, but was aware it would again change like it always does. Soon people would go back to their old ways. He hated that time, and he hated people for changing so much. Two-faced is what he would call them; although not to their face.

The day before the change Pete walked around and chatted with people at a local bar.

"So how's everything going mayor?" asked Tom Tetanuga.

"Oh, fine, I've got some planning to do for a new school."

"Well, what about the mall and casino?" suggested Tom, "You know we need 'em and it would be good for our town."

Tom was one of Pete's close friends. He and Pete would often be found at the golf course along with their other friend, Zach. Tom was Pete's right-hand man for his job. Although they remained friends, Tom worked for Pete.

"Yeah, I know Tom, those will all come in due time, but education should come first."

"Come on, you have already built a new elementary school."

"I have already stated what I am planning to do."

Tom shook his head and took another drink from his pint.

Even though the town, Winfield, was small, it got recognition from around the country as one of the best. Last year, Winfield was voted "Best Place to Live" by CFNA for the third year in a row, and Mayor Pethaford was called Mayor of the Year in his larger region for three straight years. He won the award by not always following what the people wanted, but instead went for important things like schools, police stations, and hospitals, along with the payroll increases.

Tom became serious and, closing his eyes, thought hard for the right thing to say. Then he opened them and spoke in a caring tone, but this speech seemed like it was made many times.

"Pete … we have been friends for a while, and you know …"

"It's not that speech again is it?" stated Pete in a somewhat harsh tone. "Look, I think you guys are blind and need to look at yourself. Stop looking for things that don't matter, especially when they don't need fixing."

Tom just sighed, got up, and left the bar.

Pete slammed his hand on the table and wondered when everyone would stop this nonsense. No one communicated anymore with each other and many only had a gaze that almost made him feel sorry for them. Pete understood that the outburst came from the change that people go through at the end of the week. How predictable and self-righteous! He was one of the few people who took this night for what it could be.

CHAPTER THREE

Staggering to a considerable degree, he came home late, but still recognized that none of the street lights went on. He was angry because he made sure his town had important things, let alone street lights so people could get home without getting hurt.

When he got to his house, he forced himself to the door, but halted because something didn't seem right. He opened the door and would have fallen if the door let go of him, but instead he swung around with it and nailed his hands into the wall. With the door and the wall on his hand, he was forced to wait until he was released by them.

He cried out, "I've been good! I've been good!" And with those words the door and the wall let him go, and he fell to the ground. He got back up and was about to go upstairs when he noticed the same foul smell. He thought it was strange the smell came back because he believed he got rid of it.

In great determination he moved towards the odor, but it stopped him in his tracks and threw him hard to the ground. He tried to get back up, but his head was spinning and he didn't know which way was up. Not only was he moving, but everything else was as well. The world was spinning with him.

The movement was too much for him and he gave his master what it decreed all over the floor. As he was lying on the ground he felt lost, but once his stomach seemed better, he soon went to sleep.

When he woke up, everything was still spinning for quite some time, but soon it stopped. He got up and moved about. He found himself in a strange room. As he continued to look about he noticed that he was in the kitchen; his heart froze and skipped a few beats. Although he panicked for a short while, he thought this room should be more frightening, but somehow it seemed different. He relaxed and became at ease in this room, unlike what he normally felt.

The windows were never open, so it was always dark and the little bit of light that entered the room seemed only to disappear. The light fixtures in the kitchen did not give off light anymore because he stopped changing the bulbs. Pete use to replace them, but the bulbs would burn out in a day or so. Sometimes they would even explode.

The strong smell he noticed the other day was not here anymore, or at least it was a lot less pungent. He couldn't pinpoint the location of the distant scent, but felt he better leave the kitchen and go to his bedroom. When he walked out of the room, he congratulated himself for his courage in being in the kitchen and not running away.

As he was going to his room to sleep, he observed that his whole house smelled a little funny, but didn't care because he was weary and his head pounded.

CHAPTER FOUR

When he awoke the next day, he noticed that the sun was mostly covered. He felt a little better from what he was experiencing the other day, but he stopped. He put his head down on his pillow and groaned. Pete remembered that today is the day he dreaded. He had to lay on his bed for a while because the pain of what was to come today was pumping throughout his whole body. His whole body was shaking, not with fear or pain, but with anger. He grabbed his pillow and pounded his fist into it.

Once he forced himself to get up, it wasn't so bad, but he was kind of dizzy from getting up in a haste. He thought for a moment what he would do today, but nothing came to him for a while. He had to think long and hard for what he was supposed to do today, but after a few moments it came to him. The festival was coming up soon. He needed to prepare for it.

Realizing his error, he laughed because the festival wasn't for another couple months. He thought maybe he was laboring too hard on his work and needed to take it a little easier. Pete got up and got ready for the day.

He walked around his house passing through all the mess of it, trying to think of what else he forgot. He looked around at his house and noticed that he wasn't keeping it up very well, which was odd for him. Pete, trying to kept his mind off of the painful things that would come today, did so by cleaning his home.

First, he went to the living room and then to the family room, which was the dirtiest because he stayed there the most. Then he went to the hallway which is adjacent to the front door and cleaned that part well. He then went upstairs and cleaned the couple of rooms there.

After he was finished, he noticed it was 11 am. Pete looked outside and realized it was dark and rainy. He thought it was strange that he would clean his house for around 2 to 3 hours straight. He checked the calendar and noticed that it was still the same day that it should be.

After checking the calendar, Pete then walked around his house and got angry that it wasn't any cleaner than when he first awoke. He knew he did a good job with cleaning his house, but it was still dirty! He realized he must have been in a dream once again, or maybe just moved to a dream, but he couldn't be sure.

Now he had a whole day to do what he wanted, but wished it was yet another day since he had so much free time. Instead, he had today, which was the dreaded day on which no one was around to keep him company. He sat in his chair and felt isolated from the world, and he thought about the wasted life people had.

He turned on the TV and watched a football game. It seemed that college football was on, and after a few moments the game had his whole attention. He noticed that the people on the screen started to get fuzzy, and soon it seemed like they popped out from the screen. He quickly shook his head and then the doorbell rang.

Pete guessed he was tired, so he was dozing off, but he at once got up to answer the door. When he made his way to the door, he opened it with hesitation. There was a blinding light outside, so Pete initially shielded his eyes. It took a couple minutes for him to become reacquainted with the outside world.

Before him was what he thought to be the milkman, but only for a second, and then it was someone else. Pete looked at the person, but couldn't make them out because he was too dizzy and groggy to tell. As his head stopped spinning, he noticed that the guy was in white, and he was making some type of noise. He stepped closer to the thing in white to hear what it was saying, but instead noticed it was snickering at him. Soon, this person was laughing straight into his face and took all the breath out of him. As Pete looked for this thing's face, he couldn't find any, but only a black endless void that surrounded where this person's face should be.

Pete took an even closer look at this person, and he noticed that this thing really wasn't covered in white, but instead a light red that was dark around the neck. He also noticed that this person carried a foul smell that was so familiar to him.

CHAPTER FIVE

Pete could still hear the sound of the person laughing as he woke up to a man speaking to him. He would have yelled if the person he encountered didn't try to calm him down. This person said his name a few times like he knew him, and soon Pete noticed that the person speaking to him was a man in white. Pete at once panicked, but soon realized this person was only the milkman.

He remembered about his dream and how that person changed from the milkman to something else. The moving picture haunted Pete, but he shrugged it off.

It took all his effort, but Pete looked at the man he feared.

Hey, he thought, *it is only my friend the milkman.*

The milkman, Fred, saw the uncertainty and fear in Pete's eyes so he calmly said, "Hey Pete, how's it going?"

Fred looked into Pete's eyes for a second and those eyes were blank, and then Fred looked lower down him.

Pete looked into Fred's eyes and saw the comfort he was looking for, but also recognized something else he didn't want to see.

Pete said, "Ah … I'm … ah …" and that was all he could get out because his head was hurting and Pete turned away to take something for his headache.

As he turned, Fred said in a somewhat joking voice, "must have been one heck of a dream."

That statement shocked Pete, and he at once noticed that his pants were wet. He was very embarrassed and ran to the bathroom where he felt safe from the world. As he was running away, he heard laughing. By the time he got to the bathroom, the laughing became more hysterical. To dim the sound, he yelled all the way to the bathroom, slammed the door, and turned on the light. Pete was trying to clean himself when he caught someone come to the door and then they stopped.

Pete could pick up a familiar sound through the door, but he didn't want to listen right now. He was trying to keep himself busy by cleaning himself, but still perceived a few words like, "come back…are you…wrong…milk". When he heard the word milk, he listened to this person because maybe they had a good reason to be by the door right now.

"Come on, Pete! Come out! I said I was sorry! I didn't know! Anyways, I will leave the milk here! Ahm … goodbye."

Pete wasn't sure why he acted that way to Fred, but he thought it might be because of his dream and then urinating on himself. He calmed down soon after that and came out to clean up the mess he made. When he came out of the bathroom, his heart was pounding as he came to the scene of the incident. He began to search for the mess he made but couldn't find it. He only went on his pants, but as he inspected his pants, they were clean too!

Pete ran to his front door and in a haste opening it, looking outside for where the milkman might be. Not spotting him, Pete went back inside and sat down. As he was sitting for a while, Pete later remembered that the milkman always comes on the day he hates. He, also, is one person who changes on these particular days, and that might have something to do with what just happened. He only hoped that the milkman wouldn't spread the word with how he acted.

Now he sat on the couch, and taking a pen and paper, prepared for the meeting he would have tomorrow. Pete prepared for what he would say and how he would say it. Along with preparing for the meeting, he reminisced about the past elections, and

realized he needed to get ready for the next one.
After an hour, he drifted off to sleep from boredom.

CHAPTER SIX

Pete was walking around his house staring at the floor. There was this horrible musty aroma that surrounded him throughout the whole house.

As he thought about it, the odor was much worse than before. Like the last times, the smell was so bad it made him sick and stagger. He reached a room where it was dark, and without knowing it, he was in the kitchen.

The kitchen had, by far, the worst of the scent. The smell not only surround him, but engulfed and reached deep inside him. He fell to the floor and laid there. Pete wanted to yell, but his insides wouldn't let him.

After a few moments, he stood up, but he realized there was something else in the room.

Startled, he looked around for what he feared and saw something in the corner. It was the thing he noticed before in white! It looked like its clothing was floating off the ground; the red stains around its neck was glowing deep red. He looked into the eyes of the thing, but again could only see blackness like before.

Although this thing was creeping towards him and growling, Pete was frozen in his place not being able to move a muscle. Continuing to crept closer, Pete, who was sweating profusely, would have yelled if possible.

As the creature drew near, at first, it did nothing. Then it breathed a horrible stink on him, and soon the creature laughed at him, first soft, and then loud. The spit of the animal came upon the face and mouth of Pete and burned deep into his eyes and skin. It was at this moment he could turn away and run out of the kitchen. The thing was still laughing like before, but this time the sound was not only coming from the kitchen, it seemed to come from everywhere.

Pete's face was burning and he ran to the couch where he was sleeping to wake himself up. He saw himself sleeping, but when he tried to speak to wake himself up his mouth wouldn't open. In a panic he touched his own face, but couldn't find his mouth. Instead he found what seemed like blisters lining his mouth. Touching one, it popped and the pus ran down his face. Although, when he looked at his hands, he caught sight of blood all over them. Startled, he ripped his mouth open in confusion.

Pete awoke screaming and checked himself for any damage that may have come upon him. He found nothing wrong and calmed himself down by breathing slowly. He got up to check the time and it stated 6 pm. It surprised him that he slept for so long, but he got up to make sure he wouldn't go back to sleep.

As he was moving around his house, he took a deep breath to determine if the air smelled strange. Pete was thankful that the air seemed fine to him so he relaxed.

He moved to the table to get a pen and paper and wrote out what he would say the next day. The day for his speech at the festival was arriving. He crafted, "Ladies and gentleman, you know where I stand, I am not here to become friends with any of you, you know full well. I hope you understand why I must press so hard for this action as I am here for the better of my constituency. You know of my track record; I have nothing to hide. I ask that you look into your heart to change your course of action because I have a better one. I understand you are tired of me coming before you every year, but I feel that nothing would be accomplished if I didn't push you. Remember in the past when I would push for things and you wouldn't get it? I still continued to drive forward, not for me, but for the betterment of the town. This is all I have to say, but I ask that you would consider strongly what I am proposing."

After he wrote this all down, and was satisfied, he left his speech there on the table and proceeded to bed.

6048260

Pret A Manger
Aberdeen
Shop Number 293

AB25 1HJ

31/07/2017 16:34:08 21452000219
Monika Pa
POS : 2 - 1111 2

	TAKE AWAY		
1	BRIE TOMATO & BASIL BAGUET	3.15	
1	COCONUT HOT CHOCOLATE	2.75	*

INCLUSIVE TOTAL DUE	5.90
CARD	5.90

VAT BREAKDOWN

%	NET	TAX	Gross	
20.00	2.29	0.46	2.75	*

01224 62 0020
VAT No. 927137420

CLOSED 31/07/2017 16:35:09

CHAPTER SEVEN

Pethaford made his way to the fair; the whole town seemed to be at the event. Cars were parked all across the streets and in the grass. People were everywhere, and everyone seemed to be having a good time. Pethaford enjoyed giving a speech every year at this event because everyone was in a good mood, and his speech always took place at the best time of the day because everyone was still around.

He made his way through the crowd to find his right-hand man, Tom. Tom had been with Pete through thick and thin, and even though they both had a very poor meeting last time, they were all smiles.

"What's the agenda for today?" asked Tom.

"Well, I'll let these fine folks enjoy their time and probably give the speech at high noon."

"Let me see it," Tom requests.

Pete hands the speech to him and after Tom looks through it he states, "So you're really gonna go through with this?"

"I have to Tom. It's for the best and you cannot fight me."

"I'm not gonna fight ya, but you have to understand what you are doing. 'Em people are not bout to like this."

Pete gave a nice laugh at that remark and thus stated, "the people will be fine with this. They will not care like you say."

"All right, just as long as you know what you're doing. You win every year, them people love ya, but I'm just wondering if maybe this might level your great stand."

"There's a reason I win every year, and that's because I'm the best, I know what I'm doing, and I get crap done." Pete was getting pissed and he was showing it by huffing and puffing.

Tom noticed the quick change in Pete's attitude and reversed the subject to a lighter mood. Everything was going smooth until Jennifer appeared into the picture.

"Hey guys, how ya'll doing?" Jen had a huge smile and knew she could get what she wanted from anyone except the mayor since they were married. Pete and Jen broke up a year ago, but they both were too lazy, and/or busy, to get the divorce papers in order and completed.

Tom, knowing this could go poorly, quickly stepped in, "Jen, get the heck out of here!"

"Well ... that was mighty blunt and rude ... so, I was just wondering, if this man here gets elected to mayor again, can I get some of them moneys?"

"Jen, get outta here! You are not wanted and I will call the Law Enforcement for assault if ya don't leave!"

Tom was getting angry at this whole ordeal, because Tom knew if Pete got into the mix, things would get out of hand. It is unfortunate that Jen is stubborn and so she continued to push.

"So Pete, let's just make this official then and I can take all your money. Better yet, I could go to the Principal Law Enforcement and send you to jail."

Pete only blinked at the woman and calmly said, "I don't know what you are talking about. If you want to finally get the divorce papers all in order that is fine by me, but you will not get all my money. In fact, you won't get any of my money. I will fight for that in court and I will win, 'cause I always do. As far as this whole PLE thing goes, where would that get you? Why would you need the Principal Law Enforcement?"

"You know darn well why the PLE would get involved with the crap you're pulling!"

"But Jen, what are you talking about? Are you feeling okay?"

"I'm fine, but you won't be!" Jen storms off realizing that she is getting nowhere with the conversation.

Tom turns to Pete and states, "well she might be a problem."

Pete laughs, "naw, she ain't gonna be a problem. Those southern women sure are stupid though!" Tom and Pete had a good round of laughing.

Both Pete and Tom continue to talk for a while, but they move on from the stage, and walk throughout the park getting food to eat.

About noon they walked back to the stage and Pete prepared to deliver his speech.

"Well Pete," says Tom, "good luck with your speech, I sure wouldn't want to be you."

Pete makes his way on the stage, receives the mic, and does some stand-up comedy. After about ten minutes, everyone listening to the speech can be heard laughing in what seems to be one voice. Pete is killing it, and Tom knows it.

How the heck does this man do this? They love him, but why? Tom wonders.

Pete is going through his whole routine and later stops after about twenty minutes and walks off the stage.

People chant. "More, more, more, more!"

Pete comes back to the mic and begins again. "Well folks, that's all for the jokes. Now, let's get serious."

Pete goes over the speech he wrote yesterday and the crowd is on his every word. The crowd is not angry.

"…the building you all go to every week will be destroyed. This has to be done. The town will be stronger without it; the town will flourish because of it! This day you fight for honor ... for prosperity!"

In the crowd a few chuckle, but the rest are still hanging on Pete's every word, wondering why and what this means.

At once someone in the crowd yells out, "But why? Why do you have to do this? It brings you no harm."

Pete glares at the man. The man's eyes light up as if he realizes what he said. Pete continues to stare for a minute at this man and the man continues to pull back.

Pete says nothing, but at this point Tom comes up to the mic and gets the crowd going. Saying a bunch of things like, "Pete gave you all this and he can give you more if you trust him! Has he ever let you down? Has he ever lied to any of you? I say no! He has changed this town for the better! Look at our hospital. It is quickly becoming nationally known for innovative new ways to fight diseases. Or our schools, take a look at the new elementary school that was built only a couple years ago. Hasn't that been bringing in people from neighboring areas? All these things are because of this man before you. He has given you all and will continue to give you more. All you need to do is trust him."

Tom's speech was all that was needed for the crowd to become ecstatic. Not crazy with hate, but crazy with ecstasy. Pete and Tom glanced at each other and smiled. Pete reaches out his hand and takes hold of Tom's shoulder, nods his head, walks away, departing the stage. Tom follows him.

"How do you do it?"

"Do what? Tom, it was you that really got them going."

Tom and Pete turn the corner and are out of sight from the crowd. Pete turns around and grabs Tom's throat, pushing him up against a wall.

"If you ever take my spotlight again, you will pay for it Tom! Who are the people voting for? You? No! Me!"

Tom tries to say something, but he cannot.

"Yeah that's right Tom, you are speechless. That's what I wanted the crowd to be, speechless because of me. I had that one man gripping in fear. This is about fear and power and here you go trying to say all the wonderful things I have done. Would I have gotten to all of that? Yes! Give me some time to say. Okay?"

Pete releases Tom from his grip and turns towards the stage.

Pete makes a double take and turns back around towards Tom saying to him, "just get out of here, before you mess something else up. I'm doing just fine without you."

Pete goes back on the stage and continues to declare to the crowd.

Tom walks away stunned.

CHAPTER EIGHT

One month later, the building Pete spoke about in his speech was being demolished. Pete was standing and watching the demolition being done, making sure everything was going along okay.

This has to make them happy. Now they will finally be satisfied, thought Pete.

The demolition took a few days to complete, but after the building was leveled, Pete was satisfied that the job was complete. Winfield would be the first town, in all the country, to not allow the building. People would be normal, and Pete wouldn't have to worry about them changing at the end of the week.

Pete was in high spirits, knowing the day he often dreaded would not be an issue.

As Pete leaves for his home, nearing it, he goes through the gate and the grassy lawn. Pete came up to the porch and stopped at the door. Pete sniffs the air for any danger, and notes that everything seems to be clear. He steps into the house and walks around.

Sniffing the air in each room he notices that there is no odor, even a musty or stuffy smell. He then walks into the kitchen and turns on the light. Yes, that's right! The light, which had been going out, has been working for a few weeks now.

Pete walks around the kitchen, and satisfied with what he finds in this room, leaves the kitchen, and sits down on his chair, turning on the TV. The time is 3 in the afternoon.

Some sitcom is on, and Pete drifts off to sleep, but before he can completely fall asleep he awakes. Ever since that mailman incident, he has been having trouble sleeping, even though nothing has gone awry since then. Even with the lingering fear, Pete falls asleep.

CHAPTER NINE

Pete wakes to hear the doorbell go off. Panicking, he freezes and hopes they will go away, but he hears the doorbell ring once again.

This time around, he takes longer to get out of his chair and drifts to the door. He looks through the peephole and sees no one.

Afraid, he backs from the door, and is about ready to walk back to his chair, when the doorbell rings a third time.

"What do you want?" Pete asks.

There is no response for a few seconds. "For you to buy cookies." says a soft high-pitched voice.

Pete laughs at his own jumpiness and opens the door. Seeing no one, Pete looks around, and yells out again.

"What do you want?"

After hearing no response, Pete takes a step outside his door and asks again.

"What do you want?"

The door slams behind him and Pete turns around and tries to open the door, but he cannot. The door is either locked or stuck! Pete curses and turns back around to face the lawn. The sun is not out, and Pete looks at his watch to which it reads the time is 4 in the afternoon.

"The sun should still be out." Pete says to himself.

He then walks off of his deck and lands on the grass, but no, it's not grass, although, it should be. Pete sticks his hand down on the ground and feels it. Pete assumes that it is dust or dirt, but it is hard to tell. He thus turns around and is about to go up to his house, but realizes he cannot see his house either. In fact, it is impossible to see anything in this light, because there seems to be no light anywhere. Just pitch black.

Pete is troubled now, but knows he needs to find out what happened, and so he gets up and walks. He keeps his hands in front of him, hoping that he will not stumble. He walks in a slow motion, and tries to move forward, hoping that his eyes will adjust to the darkness. His eyes adjust to nothing, and Pete continues on in pitch black.

After a bit of walking, he trips and falls down, hitting his head on a nicely placed rock.

CHAPTER TEN

Pete's head is spinning and he struggles to open his eyes, but when he does he is awake in the chair. He is so happy it was just a dream! Or is this part a dream? Pete is not so sure.

Pete gets up from his chair and walks around trying to figure out what is real and what is not. He makes his way around the whole house including the kitchen and finds nothing wrong. The sun is also out! He later decides he will go to the bar because it is clear that he is in need of a drink and someone to tell this crazy dream to.

He goes to the door to open it, but it will not budge. Pete tries with all of his might, but the door will not move. Frustrated, he goes to one of his windows and looks out. Everything looks all right, so he takes a chair and swings it at the window. The window does not break. He puts his hand on the glass to feel it. *It seems real*; he thinks. Pete tries to open the window, but it wouldn't budge either. He walks to every window, door, even the attic, but nothing would open.

"Why would this be happening? I don't get it. Is this a crazy trick the town's playing on me, perhaps because I got rid of that stupid building?" Pethaford reasons out loud.

Pete is not sure what to do. Does he go to sleep? Maybe he is in the other place, the place where everything is dark? Is he stuck in some time thing? Is this punishment for something?

Pethaford knows what might be wrong, but … *of course …* he thinks … *the cell phone!* He finds his phone and tries to call, but the phone won't even turn on. Pete then runs to his land line and tries that, but it has no tone. Frustrated, he walks over to his chair, sits down, and sees his remote in front of him. He looks at it and tries to turn on the TV. *Of course it's not going to work,* considers Pete, but he tries anyway.

CHAPTER ELEVEN

The TV turns on, but the moment of excitement fades. Pete sees on the screen nothing but static. He tries to change the channel, but nothing seems to work. Disappointed, he turns off the TV, but it will not turn off. He keeps on pressing the buttons, but nothing happens. After a while, he gives up and closes his eyes. Right as he is just about to fall asleep he hears a whispered voice in his right ear.

"Hey …"

Startled, he wakes up and looks over his right shoulder, and continues to look all around him. He sees nothing, everything is normal; he is only freaking out, even if it is for good reason.

Wait a minute, Pethaford thinks. He looks at the TV and it is black now, no static. Pethaford wonders what that means and tries to change the channel, the sound, anything on the TV, but it does nothing. Giving up, he goes back to his chair and tries to sleep again. Pete is just about to fall asleep when again he hears a voice in his left ear.

"Hey …"

This time Pethaford jumps to his feet and yells out, "What do you want? What the heck do you want? Leave me alone. I have done everything. I have given you everything. What more do you need?"

Pethaford was not expecting an answer as he was only frustrated, but he got one.

"You. Your soul. Your everything."

"What? Why would I give you myself?"

"Don't you remember? I gave you everything, four years ago, and now is the time for payment."

"What payment, what happened four years …" it was at this point Pethaford remembered what happened.

CHAPTER TWELVE

Pethaford's head hurts and he tries to wipe off something on his face, but recognizes he cannot see anything. Of course, he is back in pitch black world.

Remembering he fell, he thus tries to grasp around for what might have made him stumble. He feels something a little behind him and it seems like a root. He brushes his hand along the root to the tree bark and notices he is now standing alongside the tree. Pete touches the tree and tries to go around it to see if he can find a low branch with leaves on it. He finds nothing of the sort and sits down against the tree.

Reasoning to himself, he wonders what he should do. *Does he stay here? Does he continue on? What is he supposed to do?*

Pethaford is truly in a hopeless state and has no clue what to do.

To help with the despair, he keeps on talking to himself and feels better."This is something new ..." says Pethaford out loud.

He continues to sit and talk to himself. Now, if you were walking by this man and heard him talking to himself, you would think he was crazy, and maybe he is, but there is just not much to do at this point, other than move on. For Pethaford, this is not an option, and he continues on talking to himself, trying to figure out what he is doing.

Suddenly, he is not talking to himself, as there is a small still soft whisper that comes around him. He cannot pinpoint where this sound is from, only that the voice is impossible to hear, but the voice seems to try to push through Pethaford's own thoughts.

He is not sure how to talk to this new voice, but there is something calm and peaceful about the voice. For some reason, Pethaford even wants to trust the voice, but that's just crazy, because it's a voice coming from the pitch black. One thing he knows for sure, ever since he stopped by this tree and began to ponder everything, and with hearing the voice, he has some sort of sanity back, or rest, or whatever it might be called.

Pethaford sits and talks and the voice becomes louder, but it's not only a random voice or thought. He notices that when he reflects on something, the voice will just respond to him. This voice knows his thoughts!

At this recollection, Pethaford stands up afraid and asks out loud, "who are you?"

Everything is still silent, as he is facing the tree sounding like a fool. Thinking the tree must be magical, Pethaford reaches out and touches it, but nothing happens. He then sits against the tree like before, but still nothing happens. Pete even goes as far as talking to himself for a while, hoping that the voice will talk to him, again. He now has an uneasiness about all of this. What was the voice? What am I doing? Why am I here? Pethaford panics. All peace within him is gone, and he moves on from the tree.

CHAPTER THIRTEEN

Pethaford begins, like when he first began to walk in this world, by moving carefully with both hands in front of him. He still cannot see anything, but continues on. After what seems like hours of doing this, he is now about to give up from sheer exhaustion; he hears a voice over on his right.

"Hey…"

Pethaford, in pure excitement, yells out, "yes! What is it?"

"You seem to be lost, and I can help you. Come over here, follow my voice. I will show you the way out."

Now Pethaford is so thrilled to have someone else in here with him. He cries out, "thanks so much! You cannot imagine what this means to me. I have been looking for a way out of this mess for hours."

"Oh yeah, well I know my way, just continue to follow me. You will be just fine. I promise."

So, Pethaford follows the voice and the voice continues to cry out to him.

"Yes, this way. Just a little closer. Just keep on coming. Just try to be careful. Come on now. Come. Come."

After a few minutes of this, Pethaford notices something. The voice talking to him is not the same voice as before. This is not the voice he heard sitting at the tree. In fact, there is something about this voice that worries him.

He stops and yells out to the voice, "are you sure I should be going this way? Maybe this is the wrong way?"

Pethaford hears no response and tries to turn around. Try, because he is, in fact, unable to move his legs.

He now hears the voice say in a whisper, "oh no! You must have done something wrong! You didn't go the right way! This is your fault not mine!"

"Wait, don't leave me! Help me out! Please!" yells Pethaford at the top of his lungs.

There is no response; Pethaford realizes that he made the wrong decision. He went the wrong way, the voice was trying to help him out, but he messed up. At this point, he was up to his knees in something and it was bringing him down into the earth. *I am going to die here,* determined Pethaford. *This is the end.*

He tried with all his might to move, but it was useless. There was no way to move.

Now something must be explained right here. Pethaford never cries, but Pethaford cries here, and does so as a little baby.

"Oh please, someone help me! I'm so sorry. I'm so sorry! Please just help me out of this."

He ponders and his life flashes before his eyes. After a few moments of thinking, Pethaford realizes that the whisperer is once again talking back to him. Whether he speaks out loud, or thinks in his head, the whisperer knows exactly what to say.

"Please help me! I'm sorry I didn't listen to you and got angry. Please…"

The whisperer gives him a suggestion to lean over to the left and reach out as far as he can. He does just that and low and behold, there is something to grab onto. Pethaford works with all of his arm muscle strength and gets close enough to the thing to grab onto it with his arms and legs. Working his way up the thing, he can get out of whatever he walked into.

"Now what?" asks Pethaford.

He is getting the sense that straight is the best option and does that. Once again, he moves at a slow pace along the ground, and tries to go as far as he can.

He continues on this path and when everything seems in despair, and he is so exhausted, he sees something new in this place.

"Yes! Of course! A light!" sings Pethaford.

He laughs at himself because he hasn't sung in forever.

Pethaford drifts, but with hope now. He continues along the way, towards this light, and the light becomes nearer and nearer. When he is but a few feet from the light, he notices it is but one candle in front of him. Pethaford, disappointed, looks at the candle for a while, and then picks it up. He uses the candle to look at the ground and everything around him. Then, he recognizes that the ground is a gray ashy color, and not at all pleasing to look at. He then moves to the spot to where the candle was placed and notices that there is writing on it.

One candle by itself is useless. The same can be said of two or even three candles, but when you have a bunch of candles all together, it can light up anything, even a world as cruel as this.

Wow, that is totally lame, and not at all helpful, thinks Pethaford.

And he was right, it's great, and sure it might be true, but how does that help Pethaford?

And Pethaford had this same thing on his mind. He stood there wondering what the inscription might mean. As he was trying to figure this out, he heard the whisperer speak and he, once again, listened. At one point the whisper almost takes out the light from the candle.

Moving around to the other side of the lamp stand, Pethaford is told from the same whisperer he should look over there too. When he looks at the new inscription it reads: *Lame is right, and lame is true, sit on me and you won't be a fool.*

Pethaford laughs, "it's like it knew exactly what I was thinking."

He sits on the stand, with the candle in his left hand, and waits. He thought for sure that the stand would go down or activate something, but nothing seemed to happen.

For what seems like forever, Pethaford sits and sits, and tries not to fall asleep.

Bored out of his mind, he turns his whole body to the left, and soon after back to the right, and the stand spins from the momentum that is created by the shifting of his weight. The spinning does not stop or slow down, and Pethaford is surprised it takes no effort for him to hold onto the stand.

As Pethaford is spinning on the stand, he notices something odd. He takes his candle in his right hand and puts it close to his face. The light from the candle is spreading. It is moving beyond the candle and staying in the air floating around the area. It begins to make a clear picture of what he is walking through. Every second the whole area around him becomes clearer, but what is Pethaford supposed to do?

He keeps on looking around the world and tries to see what the stand is attempting to show him. He even gets up on the stand, so he can get a better view. At that point, it hits him. There is nothing in this world: no grass, no animals, no leaves, no trees, (except if you count the tree that Pethaford already found, but he couldn't see the tree at this point.) There was nothing! Pethaford thought this was the most awful trick ever!

"What am I going to do?"

In desperation, he hangs his head down, and notices that right in front of him, on the ground, there is a reflection.

"What is that?"Pethaford jumps off of the stand, and everything around him goes dark; he lands on whatever the reflecting thing was, twisting his ankle. He cries out in pain. His right foot kills him, but there is no way to check what condition his foot might be in or what he landed on. Instead, he drifts off to sleep.

CHAPTER FOURTEEN

Pethaford awakes to the sound of the voice still continuing to talk.

"Oh, you remember what happened. You stood there yourself. I am the reason for your success and I am the reason you are the way you are. I am also the reason you will be destroyed! You will die because of me. You cannot try to escape it now. And no, you will not die the way you expect you would, you will be dead in this world and the next world. Oh...I see it in your eyes. You have already been there. Well, tell me how has it been."

"Well, um, what are you talking about?"

"You know exactly what I am talking about, there is no need to deny it now. This is you fault and you fail. You cannot succeed. You cannot beat me."

"What? This cannot be real, this has to be a joke."

"This is no joke. This is life, and your life at that."

Pethaford walked around the room and could not believe what he was hearing. This voice was telling him a bunch of insane things. There was no way that all of this was true. This was too much, but maybe this explained all the crazy things that had been happening the past months.

Pethaford walked back to his chair and froze. He now saw an image on the screen of the TV. It was the scene of him four years ago talking to himself, and saying crazy things about wanting to be the best mayor ever, and he would do anything to get there.

The voice continues to talk to Pethaford, "I cannot be too mad though, because of you I can fully take this town. You really did a great job. Well, I gave you the gift, but still, you did your service quite nicely."

This was too much for Pethaford to bear, and he fell to the floor. What has he done? Where is the spirit he had before? Where is the fight and the drive that was in him? Where was the attitude of power? Where was it now? He felt nothing. He felt empty and he didn't know what to do about it.

Pete turned around and began to talk to the TV, but the front door right next to him swung open. Pethaford approached the door and noticed that the sun was out and he heard birds. He had never been so excited about hearing the birds before, but it was nice to have sun and sound. He took a step down the stairs and put both feet on the ground. He drops to both knees to smell the grass.

"How wonderful the grass smells," thought Pethaford! "This is something I have taken for granted for oh so long."

Pete then got to his feet and began to walk around the town. He passed main street and people were out and about. He passed by the local beauty parlor, the salon, the library and he saw people were everywhere. Many people were laughing and everyone seemed to be having a good time. A few people noticed him and waved.

He walked into the bar hoping to find Tom, and he did. Tom was right in his usual spot, and when he noticed Pete he turned away.

Pete walked up to Tom and began to talk with him.

"Hey Tom, so this might sound crazy, but what day is it."

"Oh you know Pete, you don't need to get all snobbish about it already. Yes, you destroyed the building yesterday and so no one can go the building today."

Pete stopped and reflected to himself. This is the morning after. Meaning everything that happened last night only took a night, and he was still here in his town.

Now Pete had no clue what to think, but he took a seat right next to Tom. A second later Zach entered the bar and looked at Tom and Pete.

"Hey guys, of course I would see you both here. So, this is kind of sweet." Zach motions with his hand towards the window.

"Yeah," said Tom. "Everyone is out and about, doing their duty as citizens."

"Well," said Zach, "that's one way to put it, but now we can do whatever we want, we don't have to worry about that building anymore."

"And that exactly is the problem," states Tom.

"What? Tom, weren't you the one to support this? At the fair you got on the stage and was all gung-ho about it."

"True, but that was only because I was suppose too."

"Yeah that's right, it was Pete that really wanted this to be done, and done it is. So, Pete you have been quiet. What do you say?"

Pete can only look at the table. A few days ago, he would have been so sure about what he did, but now he wasn't. He did not understand what to believe anymore.

"Yeah, I'm not sure anymore..."

"What?" Tom made a hard left towards Pete and got right up in Pete's face. "Remember only a month ago when you grabbed me by the throat and threatened me? What do you mean by you don't know anymore?"

"Well, Tom it's kind of lot to tell you. I mean I had all this crap happen."

"I don't get it? Has the great Mayor Pete Pethaford lost it? What just happened to you?"

"Okay, I'll tell you both, but you will promise me not to tell anyone, and we need to go to a more private place. And once I start talking, you cannot interrupt me or ask questions till I am done."

CHAPTER FIFTEEN

Pete began to take a good hour and a half to explain everything that has been going on with him. He only left out one part, the part he got all of his success the past four years from trading his life. After Pete spoke of everything that had happened, Tom was the first to speak and laugh. Tom then looked at Zach and they laughed together. Pete stared at both of them.

"That was great Pete, the story was really epic. I can't believe you went through all of this work just to get this laugh out of us, but you had us both going."

"Um, Pete?" said Zach. "You still have it. You really do. Great story. So, guys I was thinking we should play some golf."

Pete was just staring at the table. He couldn't believe what they were saying. They weren't taking him serious.

"Tom and Zach, have I ever lied to either one of you?"

Both Tom and Zach looked at each other and laughed some more.

"Seriously Pete, funny stuff, but really we get the joke now."

"No," said Pete. "You still don't get it. This is not a joke and never was meant to be."

"What are you getting at Pete?"

"Everything I told you is true."

Now Tom and Zach had Pete's full attention.

Zach, the humorous one in the group, spoke first, "Pete, I think you are going crazy then. I mean stuff like this doesn't just happen to a person. We will have to send you to the psychiatric ward. Come on Tom, lets strap him up."

Zach cracked up at his own joke, but stopped after Tom and Pete were not laughing.

"Whoa Zach, hold on there, I think Pete is serious about this."

"No, he can't be."

"I think he is...I mean look at him. He looks worried. Honestly I haven't seen Pete like this for years. He is not acting the same way. I think he is telling the truth."

"Yeah, I don't know so much. I mean people sometimes just break down and, you know, start to have mental issues. It just happens."

"I don't think he is having a mental break down, as you would call it. He just seems worried."

Pete was just listening to them talk, but he finally spoke up. "Okay, both of you, stop. I'm not crazy, this is really happening. I'm not having a mental break down."

"Pete, how do I...how do we know that?" said Zach.

"Well," said Pete. And Pete told the story of what happened four years ago, this time including the part about selling his life.

After finishing the rest of the story Zach speaks up. "This seems like some kind of crazy movie. This seems like a horror film. This stuff just doesn't happen to everyday people. So Pete, what you're saying is that you sold your soul to get success out of this life?"

"Yes."

"Well, it looks like you got a pretty good deal. I mean you got everything you wanted, and you sure are successful, but really man, this whole selling a soul just doesn't make much sense."

"It doesn't make sense to me either, it's just how it is. Listen, I don't like this, but what can I do? I have to figure out what is going on."

Tom and Zach looked at each other for the hundredth time and there was nothing they could say. "This man is crazy," is the look both of them seemed to be giving each other.

"So what do you want us to do?"

"I don't know, I just figured I should tell someone. How about this, you both come to my house and maybe then you can see what happens?"

Zach looked right at Pete, smiled and said, "it's a date, we'll come over tomorrow."

CHAPTER SIXTEEN

It was a quarter to whenever Tom and Zach were suppose to come over. Pethaford was concerned that he would go to the new world before either came over and was concerned because it seems to happen when he falls asleep. The crazy thing is, when he went to bed last night, he didn't go to the other world.

He paced around the house. Looking at his watch every ten seconds, he was hopeful they would show up early.

When it was fifteen minutes before they should show up and their was still no sign of them, he looked out his window every few seconds, hopeful they were just around the corner.

Finally he heard a knock at the door. Pethaford sighed, being very thankful and walked over to the door to opened it.

There in front of him was Tom.

"Hey, so I was gonna bring flowers over for you, hoping that it would help you feel better."

Tom was laughing at his own joke, but Pete was not that thrilled.

"I'm just glad you are here. Come in."

Tom just continued to look at Pete.

"You know Pete, I don't think I will."

"What. Why?"

"Well, why would I when you are still asleep?"

"Tom, you're making no sense, and this isn't very funny."

"No man, I'm serious, look over there."

Pete looked over to where Tom was pointing and sure enough, someone was on his chair, sleeping.

"I don't remember him being there."

Pete and Tom walked over to the chair to see who was there. When they got to the chair they were shocked at what they saw.

"Zach? But Tom, this doesn't make any sense at all."

Sure enough, Zach was on the chair sleeping away."

"This doesn't make any sense. Tom, I swear, he wasn't in here before you got here."

Tom was just looking at Pete in odd bewilderment.

"So, what's going on then? Wait, this is just a joke you are both playing. Happens all the time in movies."

Pete went over to Zach and shook him. Zach did not move. He once again began to shake Zach and started to yell in his face.

"Wake up Zach! What the heck are you trying to pull?"

At this point Pete was exhausted from not sleeping, and even when he did, it was not sound sleep. Therefore, Pete was not sure if he was in a dream.

Around this point Pete was hitting and punching Zach, but Zach still did not move. Eventually, Tom stopped Pete and said to him, "He will not respond, can't you tell?"

"What the heck are you pulling Tom? A person does not just fall asleep and stay asleep like this. I don't know what's going on, but this is what I was talking about. There have been a lot of crazy things happening at this house."

Pete's nerve broke again, and he started to personally attack Tom. It began as yelling and having it out at each other. Then the argument escalated to fighting. They began to struggle with one another, and were bumping into things all over the room, breaking things. Tom got the upper hand on Pete and picked him up and threw him against the window. Pete landed against the window and hit the floor. He went unconscious, but this was not what got Tom's attention.

"What the heck?"

He walks over to the window. *There is no way that the window should not have shattered after that,* thought Tom. Tom doesn't think much more about it, but instead walks over to the door.

He reaches to open the door, but it would not budge.

"Now what's going on?"

Tom walks around the rest of the house and tries to open every door and window. He then proceeds to Pete to wake him. Pete wakes up after a few moments and is staring right into Tom's face.

"Get up! Get up! Get up!"

Pete was moving and shrugging his shoulders. He grabbed his right shoulder with his left hand and massaged it.

"I told you, I'm not playing a game." Pete said, as he was still on the ground and was covering his eyes with his right hand.

Tom, still frustrated, squats in front of Pete and says, "I cannot get out of the house. The doors are locked and nothing will open."

"Yeah, we are now going through what I went through a few days ago."

"Well, what do we do?" Tom sits down on the floor.

"Die..."

"Haha Tom," said Pete sarcastically, "no need to be funny."

Suddenly, Zach was right in front of both Pete and Tom. Zach then begins to speak.

"Hey guys. How are you doing? What are you both doing over here? Why are you both on the floor?

Are you okay Pete? What happened to you? Hey guys, I had the best sleep ever. Why are you looking at me like that? What is your problem?"

Tom spoke first, "Zach, you were completely asleep just a little bit ago."

"Hmm, what are you talking about?"

Pete and I found you asleep just a little bit ago. You were on the chair and you didn't respond to me at all.

"Oh? Well, that's odd."

"Yeah it is, so what do you remember?"

"Nothing."

"Really? So what happened before you got to the chair Zach?"

Both Tom and Pete were looking at the ground during most of the talk, but now Tom turned towards Zach, but Zach wasn't there.

"Wait, now where did he go?"

Pete, in pain, strained to look over at where Zach should have been and he didn't see him either. Pete's head felt like it was ready to explode and he blacked out.

CHAPTER SEVENTEEN

Pete woke up and quickly got to his feet, but soon fell to the ground again. Pete was once again in pitch black, and his ankle was killing him. It felt like forever since he was in the world and he couldn't remember what he did last. He sat and tried to clear his mind. *What was I doing before I was on the ground,* thought Pete? He sat in silence for the longest time. He could not remember what he was doing.

"Door..."

Pete freaked out for a second because the sound came out of nothing.

What about a door? he thought. He tried hard to remember just what a door had to do with this.

One candle by itself is useless. The same can be said...

After remembering this, it came to him. He had just jumped off of the candle stand and landed on the door handle. That's why his foot was killing him.

He began to search around for the door. After a few moments, he found the door, and then the door knob. He turned the doorknob and half expected the door not to open. The door didn't open.

"Darn it," said Pete out loud.

Then he realized that he was sitting on the door and got up off it.

The door did not budge easily, but eventually the door swung open. Pete wasn't sure what to do now. The door was open, but how does he do anything in the darkness?

Pete sat down, not sure of what to do.

A light was coming from inside the door. He couldn't be sure how far the light was, but one thing was for sure: the light was moving towards him.

As the light got closer he could tell there was someone holding a light.

"Who is there?"

The person did not respond to Pete.

"Stop! Don't come any closer. Who are you?"

The person holding the light still did not stop. At this point, he was only a couple hundred feet away from Pete.

Pete tried hard to see who this person was. He couldn't see his face. He then noticed that there was blood on this person, and that was enough for Pete to slam the door closed.

Pete's heart was jumping out of his chest. He was panicking and unsure of what to do, so he slammed the door close.

He then heard a knock on the door.

"Who is it?"

"A friend"

"Who?"

"Your friend."

Pete still wasn't sure what to think, but something about the voice gave him enough reason to trust this person. All he knew was that Pete was really starting to hate doors.

"How do I know you're a friend?"

"Because you need me."

"Why should I trust you? How can I?"

"You can only open the door to find out. I cannot force you, I can only invite you."

The more he talked, the more he wasn't sure, but maybe he was just trying to talk himself out of opening the door.

He sat in silence for a while, thinking and trying to figure everything out. The same whisper he heard awhile back suddenly came through his head.

He felt the same peace even though he was afraid, and so he opened the door.

Light blasted through and blinded Pete. He quickly lost his balance and fell into the opened door. He was expecting to feel the pain of landing on the ground, but he felt none of that.

He opened his eyes and he was in a large corridor. The ceilings went up a hundred feet high and reddish light came from all around. He saw large beams holding up the ceilings. On those beams were intricate carvings of various creatures.

Pete tried to look around, but he couldn't. All he could do was look ahead.

In the left corner of his eye, he could see a figure. Someone was with him. They began to walk. *Who was this?* That was all Pete could think.

As Pete continued to walk, he came up to an extremely large door. The door was made of wood and had the same types of images that were on the beams.

The large door opened and Pete and the person to his left walked in. Pete stood at the entrance to the door watching what was happening.

There was some kind of creature in the middle of the room. It was the same type of creature that was on the beams and the door. The creature took one look at Pete, and the creature had a wicked smile on his face.

Everything that took place appeared to happen in slow motion and it felt surreal. The person who came with him, jumped a good twenty feet in the air and suddenly had a sword in his hand. He went crashing down into the creature and both of them went through the floor. It seemed like endless noise, but finally there was silence.

Pete walked over to the edge of the hole and looked down. All he saw was an endless black. Nothing as far as the eye could see. As Pete continued to look down he had shivers run along his spine.

I need to get out of here! thought Pete.

He walked around the room and saw no way out.

"This seems to be a theme in my life," sighed Pete.

He went through the same way he came from, along the corridor and past the beams. He walked up the stairs to the door. Half expecting the door not to open he hesitated for a second and then opened the door.

While still traveling through the door, he heard a voice.

"Hurry!"

"Who? Me?" said Pete.

"Be quiet! They will hear you."

"Who will hear me?"

"Stop with the questions and follow me. We are not safe here."

Pete noticed the whisper had a body. A pleasant, but fearful smile was on the face of this person. This person turned around and began to walk.

"We don't have much time. Follow me."

Pete followed the footsteps in the darkness and did everything this person said. After a good amount of walking they passed from the ash, dusty ground to grass. Right before they got to the grass, this person told him to step up.

Now they were passing along trees and Pete could hear a stream in the distance. Then Pete stopped, because he could hear other noises in the distance as well. It took him a while to realize what they were, but he was hearing crickets, an owl, a wolf, and even the sound of the wind blowing through the trees.

It also took Pete a few seconds for him to realize that he was once again alone.

"Hey! Where did you go?"

Pete looked around and noticed he could see a little in this darkness. He looked up. The moon was full and very bright.

Now what? thought Pete.

At this point he wasn't even sure which way he was originally going, and he didn't want to go back where he came from, so he sat down next to a tree. This tree, like the tree before, was bare, but Pete did not give it much thought. Soon Pete fell asleep.

CHAPTER EIGHTEEN

He awoke to the sound of laughing.

"You can't catch me. I'm way too fast for ya! Haha!" said what sounded like a girl.

Pete panicked and got to his feet.

"No way! You're too slow!"

Pete looked around for where the voices continued coming from. He gathered that they came from behind, and he turned around. He saw no one and was disappointed, but all together worried.

Standing in silence, he was about ready to sit back down when he heard whispering.

"What should we do?" said the girl.

"Shush!" said the boy in a harsh tone. "He can probably hear us."

He heard a rustle, and then realized it was them running away.

"Wait!" Pete yelled as loud as he could, but the steps only went on faster.

Pete waited for a second and soon began to walk the way the steps went away to. He wasn't sure what he just experienced, but thought that there was a possibility he was crazy. He walked through thick woods and reached a stream. Pete bent down and took water in his hands.

Continuing on his way, he crossed the stream and moved through the forest. He walked for what seemed like hours and still had no sight of anything. After moving through the thick forest, he caught sight of a clearing up ahead. He stepped through the last bit of trees and noticed a pasture. For as far as the eye could see, there was a clear field of grass. After taking a few steps in the plain, he looked back and sighted the large forest behind him. He walked some more, but grew too tired to walk and laid down in the pasture.

At this point, Pete felt helpless. He didn't understand what to do and once again he was lost and confused. He began to think about everything that was going on with him. *What was this world trying to tell him? What was happening to him? Who was that person who led him through the corridor? Who was the man who led him out of the darkness? What, where, and who were those laughing children?*

Pete began to feel hopeless. *What was he missing?*

"Can't I just have a clear answer? Can't it be known to me what is going on?"

Pete closed his eyes and sulked.

"I'm just pathetic!" yelled Pete. "I can't do anything right. I'm hopeless; just leave me al…"

Pete stopped because he wasn't sure who he was talking to, or even what he was talking about. All he knew is that he was alone, and he needed help.

Pete turned over on his side and was about ready to close his eyes and fall asleep when he noticed the grass was depressed. Not thinking too much about it, he reached out his hand to touch the grass. The depression moved back, and he could hear the slow sound of grass brushing up against something.

"Is that you? I don't suppose you would speak?"

Not expecting to hear back, he turned over to his other side.

"You know, if it helps, there are many hopeless people that come through here. They are just like you." It was the same girl he heard before; he was sure of it.

"What are you talking about? Why can't I see you?"

"I'm not sure, but it happens to everyone. It even happened to me, although I can't remember it, but I'm told it did."

"You don't talk like you are just a girl."

"How do you know I'm a girl? You have never seen me, have you?"

"No, I assumed that you were. Plus, you were playing tag with that boy."

"How do you know that was a boy?"

Pete stopped for a second. This girl or lady, or whatever you call it, was right. He wasn't sure of anything anymore.

"Will I ever be able to see you?"

"In time you will."

"Will you help me find my way?"

"I can't do that. Find your own way, but I warn you, if you do, you will only get lost."

"That makes little sense. How do I find out what or even where I am going?"

"You can't, you just … well Pete, you have to do what you did at the tree, the candle stand, or in the underground passageway."

"How do you know my name?"

The girl laughed, "oh Pete, I know more than your name."

"Are you a god or something? Are you a higher being?"

The girl laughed again, "I am not, and I guess you could call me a guide, although I can't help you."

"You are useless."

"Pete, one day you will understand, but today is not the day."

"So what now?"

He waited for a while to hear a response, but the girl seemed to have left him. He was once again alone. Pete was still lying on the ground. He wasn't sure what he was missing. All this sitting around and waiting was getting him nowhere, so he stood up and looked around. He could go through this plain and see where that leads or he could go back through the forest and follow the stream he found earlier.

Pete did not want to go over the open plain, with the hot and bright sun high overhead, so he went back to follow the stream. As he was entering the forest, the shade of the trees felt great.

Definitely a good idea, thought Pete.

He made his way to the stream and followed it downstream. He noticed that the stream was crystal clear. As he walked along the ground, he recognized a sound of an animal in front of him: a frog. Hearing the frog, he was so ecstatic he got right up to the ground to look for it.

Now this was a sight to observe because Pete, a grown man in nice well kept clothes, was on his knees looking for a frog. For even a brief moment, Pete smiled and seemed to be happy. He followed the noise of the frog, but couldn't see it. He was sure the frog was right in front of him.

"It must be invisible like the boy and girl. This really is a strange world."

He continued down the stream and realized that the trees were becoming sparse. Also, the ground was becoming less grassy, and there were patches of dirt intermingled. He then looked at the water and noticed that it wasn't crystal clear anymore. Pete stopped. He wasn't sure if he was going into the other part of the world that he started in.

This must be another side of the world, thought Pete.

He continued on, but he began to stumble. He looked up and there was no sun or moon.

The sun must have gone down and there must be cloud cover, Pete determined.

At this point he had no way to continue on, so he sat down by the stream and fell asleep.

CHAPTER NINETEEN

A rustle, a crack, a scream sounded, but it seemed to be in the distance. There was a faint sound that didn't seem to come from anywhere close by, but it sure startled Pete from his sleeping.

He sat up, looked around, but couldn't see anything. The first thought was that he went blind. He couldn't make out anything, but he could hear noises all around; whispers, and the worst part is that they knew he was here.

Over here...no over here...hey, are you lost? Can you see? Don't be afraid, for I am with you. Always. Why listen to him? Listen to me. I know what is best, and I care for you.

Pete stumbled around; the voices went on coming from all around him, but although his dream had them coming from the distance, at this point in time, the whispers were all around him.

As he was stumbling around, he tripped over a tree root, and landed in water, face first. His head was underwater, but the voices were still prevalent. He tried to swing his legs back down and touch the bottom of the water, but he couldn't feel it. He brought his head above the water and realized he was moving down stream. The only good news, Pete could think of, was that the voices were gone.

Hc began to tread water and keep the head perpendicular to the flow of stream. As he swam, he noticed that the stream was getting stronger. He swam faster hoping to reach the edge of the river, but it seemed to be of no hope.

The water was picking up too much speed at this point and 'thump,' he hit something with his head. He could feel blood coming out of his forehead, and he got light headed. As he was floating farther down the river he was losing consciousness.

Pete had no hope and at this point began to have a conversation like the desperate conversation last time.

Soon, Pete was talking to himself, and this would be a funny moment to watch or listen, but for Pete, he was alone.

"What! You don't want to talk to me now? Yeah, when I actually need help of course. Guess I'm just gunna die out here." Pete was screaming hysterically.

After swallowing water and yelling, Pete passed out.

CHAPTER TWENTY

Pete felt a kick to his side and a lighter kick to the head. He woke up and moaned.

"He's awake! What should we do?"

The voices were talking to each other. There must have been a few of them. Pete tried to see at who was talking to him, but it wasn't possible.

"I'm not sure. He could be a spy!"

"Look at him though. This guy looks awful." This was the third voice to talk, and it was a surprising sound. Something he hasn't heard in a while. It was a grown female voice.

Pete looked at the direction the people were speaking, and begged, "please help me, I'm completely lost and do not understand where I am. Plus, I cannot see anything. Are you guys visible?"

The second voice, a deeper, intimidating voice yelled out, "don't speak! We are trying to figure out if you are worth dealing with."

The female voice suddenly started talking. "Listen you. You could get us in a lot of trouble. We are not suppose to be dealing with your kind. We are just suppose to let you be. They all think you should be killed and that you are a spy. I think you are telling the truth and are just lost, but don't speak or your luck might change!"

The first voice again spoke, "see though, he's crazy, he asks if we are visible. Well, don't you guys see? He is out of his mind!"

The female voice spoke again. "Actually, he is not! I have been told of the invisible people. They hide, are unseen, and only rarely speak. My father met one a few years ago."

"So what happened?"

"I don't know. I haven't seen my father since. He spoke of this voice he heard one day, the next day he left, and then I haven't seen him since."

"Hmm, sounds like your father was crazy Amy." said the second voice in a joking manner.

In the darkness Pete could see nothing, but he heard a quick thump, and a sound of a man groaning in pain. Then a loud smack and the sound of that person hitting the ground with a loud thud.

"Yeah, what are you saying now? Huh? What's that? Look at your pathetic body on the ground. Who's laughing now? Get up! You piece of crap!

Nobody talks about my father like that!" The woman was screaming. She was kicking the guy on the ground because Pete could make out the continued thumping.

"Okay Amy, that's enough of that."

"Yeah, guess he's had enough because he's the one on the ground and passed out." Now it was Amy giving a mocking laugh.

"Well, I don't know about you, but if this person we found heard some voices, like my father, he's not crazy and he's telling the truth. Moreover, I'm gonna help him, and if you try to stop me, or even pull a move on me, you will be on the ground too. Got it?"

The first person laughed at this. "I have no problem with any of this. If you say he's safe, then that's good enough with me. Let's get him to safety though; we have been out here way too long."

"Yes, you are right with that. If he is hearing voices, I think it means he is important for some reason."

"Let's just hope that the damned do not find him."

"Let's not think about that."

The two people kneel next to Pete and help him up. He is led by both of them, one on each arm, all the way through this world. He has no clue where he is, where they are leading him, and he cannot make out where he is going.

Finally Pete asks, "how do you both understand where you are going; I can see nothing."

"Oh, that's easy, we are not blinded like you." said the first voice.

"What do you mean I'm blinded?"

The woman laughs. "You must have been in the other world? The dark world. Well, um, what's your name?"

"Pete."

"Well Pete, you have a nasty head injury, and you seemed to have lost your sight because of it. It's daytime right now. Don't worry though, we will lead you the right way."

"How do I know you are leading me the right way? In that 'dark world' you speak of, I picked up many voices, and not all of them were trying to help me."

"Pete, we are all you got, so we can either leave you here, or you can come with us."

Pete knew full well he had no chance of being by himself, so he continued on with the two people leading him.

After a point of walking, Pete got so light-headed and unaware of anything that was going on, that he began to be dragged by these two people instead of walking. Eventually, Pete just passed out.

CHAPTER TWENTY-ONE

Pete awoke to the sound of no noise, and he got up off what he was on and fell on the ground. He still couldn't see, but Pete once more got up and tried to walk around seeing where he was at. He bumped into everything including chairs, tables, and some lamp. Finally, he found the door and reaching it, opened it, took one step and fell down the stairs.

When he reached the bottom of the stairs, he scratched his head. He could feel a bandage on his forehead. He then felt around for where he was at; it was still another room. He stumbled around this room until he heard a voice.

"You had enough?"

Pete stopped and looked toward where the voice was.

"I just had to be sure of where I was. Plus, I need a glass of water."

This was the same woman that rescued him in the forest and she responded, "okay, I am going to set a few things straight. First, don't leave the room again. Second, I will get you what you need, you do not need to get it yourself, especially in your state. Third, you lie to me again, I will kill you … just like I killed that guy in the forest."

Pete froze at that and sat on the ground because of his lightheadedness.

The woman was laughing, "he is dead, but he deserved it. Don't worry though, I probably won't kill you. That would be too easy anyways. Okay, so let's get you back to your bed."

As she was getting Pete to his bed, a door swung open and a man yelled.

"They're coming! Get out! Get out! Amy!"

"I'm up here, and we're coming now!"

"Who's coming? What's happening?" asked Pete.

"The damned! We need to go now!"

Amy took Pete by the arm and pulled him down the stairs.

At the bottom of the stairs was the same man that Pete heard in the forest.

"Amy, leave that guy, he will just slow you down. In fact, he might be the reason they came here."

It was at this point that Pete realized who this was. It was the first person.

"No, we're not leaving him. He must be important then, and I will not be the one to get him killed."

"Have it your way, but I'm not coming with you then. You're on your own."

The man ran out the door and Amy and Pete were once again alone.

"Come on," said Amy. "Let's go."

Amy had to drag Pete outside. Pete was waiting to hear the sound of gunfire, but instead heard screaming from all around him. The whole town seemed to be in a frenzy.

They ran in a certain direction, and Pete wished he could ask what was going on, but instead he had to use all of his strength just to keep up.

Amy was weaving in and out of trees trying to get away from the destruction. When it seemed like they made it far enough away from the commotion, she stopped.

"Okay, Pete, do you know which direction you came from?"

"I don't know. I'm blind remember?"

"No, I mean which way were you walking when we found you?"

"I was following a stream down south. That is if the sun is in the same location as it is in my world."

"What do you mean your world?"

"I'm not from around here. I got here a few days ago and now I seem to be stuck here."

"Pete, that is how all of us got here. We all lived in the world you came from, and now we are all here.

We are not sure why we are here, but what we do know for certain is that there is a dark, dark evil here. An evil you cannot imagine."

"Is that what the damned are?"

"No, I believe the damned are people that are taken over by the evil. They are attacking my village now, and they will destroy the whole village. They cannot be stopped, and they have certain powers that are beyond anyone's imagination."

"So, how do these damned get taken over?"

"I'm not too sure, but I think they were once one of us. I also know the evil parade themselves as something great. Usually they communicate in the dark and they seem to be invisible. My father told me they are like voices in the darkness, trying to help you, but are only there to deceive."

Pete realized a connection and stated, "Amy that is exactly what happened to me. Except there was this other voice I heard that actually helped me out."

"Yeah, that's what my father heard too. It's the voice that he tried to find. He told me it wasn't going to be easy, and then the next day, I guess, he left and went to find the voice."

"This makes little sense though: why voices, why these damned, why are we in this world? This is all plain silly. I just wanna go back to being the Mayor."

"This all seems silly, but if you think about it, we are experiencing something beyond us, beyond our realm. Even if you think this is all stupid or pointless, it doesn't matter, because it is happening right now.

You are a part of it, and you cannot get out of it. Everyone that is here now cannot go back to the world we once knew."

"Okay, fine, I get it, but what are we supposed to do? You lost your village, as you say, so we are left with nothing. Now what?"

"How am I supposed to know? I'm in the same spot as you. I would say that the only thing we can do is find the voice, um the good one I guess." Amy puts her hand to her face and sighs. "You're right, this is all so stupid. Maybe we should just give up."

"Yeah, we should probably just give up."

"Yeah, there's nothing we can really do."

"Yeah, there's really nothing we can do. I agree."

Amy sits down, and takes Pete's hand, and pulls him to the ground.

Both Amy and Pete sit in silence for a while, and Pete just thinks about what is going on with everything. He thinks to himself.

Why is this all happening? Why now? What is he suppose to do? Why can't he see? Who is this Amy person?

As Pete thinks to himself, he hears a voice around him.

"I can help you both. All you have to do is follow me. You both look scared and I'm sorry for that, but just follow me. Everything will be okay."

Pete hears Amy begin to get up, and he grabs her arm.

"Don't!" He whispers quietly to her. "That voice is not right. That voice lied to me before."

Amy pulls his hand away.

Amy seeming to have forgotten that a voice just spoke said, "How do I know you are telling the truth? How do I know that you aren't just making up this crazy stuff about voices? How do I not know you aren't a damned?"

"I cannot prove anything to you. You just have to trust me. Amy, you said yourself that your father heard the voice and followed it the next day. Do you believe he was making that up?"

"No, I don't. I believe him, but isn't that why we should follow this voice and see where it leads us?"

Pete moves right to Amy's ear and whispers, "Amy, this voice we cannot believe, it has lead me down the wrong path more than once. We need to go. We have to resist."

"Alright, so what do we do?"

"I think we need to go back the way I came. We need to find the river I came down and head the opposite way from which I came. Do you know where the river would be?"

"There is only one river."

Amy grabs Pete's hand and takes him to where she found him. Along the way, Pete and Amy hear voices all around them, talking to them, tempting, and pursuing. They both continue to speak to each other and try to show what and who is real. When they reached the place where Amy found Pete, they stopped.

"Pete, this is where I found you. The river is running the same way you were facing when we found you. My guess, we follow it south where it leads upstream."

"Yeah, that's what I already told you. Let's go before the voices get to us."

It was at this moment that Pete had a strong desire to fight and kill. He wasn't sure where this emotion was coming from, he only knew it was a new emotion for this world. He wanted revenge for all that had been happening to him, he wanted someone to pay.

CHAPTER TWENTY-TWO

Amy and Pete were walking along the stream, and Amy wondered who this person she was leading was. *Was he telling the truth about everything? Was he someone she could trust?*

There was one thing she knew for sure, the voices were real. Amy just wasn't sure that Pete had heard the voices correctly; what if they weren't leading them astray? She only felt she had to get away from her village and this direction seemed like a good way to go. The only problem was that many people did not venture this way. By continuing this way, she was going just about as far as she had ever come.

The stream was more like a river, wide as the eye could see, and it was moving quick. Amy was tempted to push Pete in the river. She was almost being beckoned to. The voices in her head were telling her so, but she understood (at least she hoped she knew) that these voices were only messing with her. Amy would have considered she was crazy had she known these voices were not hers. But maybe they were her own voices?

It's not like I haven't killed anyone before. What would be the difference this time?

When she led Pete up the stream, there was almost no grass. There was just a type of dirt, except the dirt had a grayish tint to it, almost like it was ash. Amy knew the damned had been to this area because everywhere she looked she saw that everything was dead or dying. The sun was even darker in this area and it was colder, almost like the sun was being blocked by something.

"Pete?"

"Yeah?"

"When you came into this world, what do you remember seeing?"

"Not much, it was dark and I could barely see anything. I don't remember any grass and there was almost no sound except for the voices I heard."

"What was on the ground instead of grass?"

"It was hard to tell, but it seemed to have been dirt. There was nothing living around except this one tree in the middle of nowhere."

"Hmm..."

"Why, what are you thinking?"

"Well, this area here has almost no grass and a dirt or ashy colored ground. The sun seems to be dimmed and it seems to be colder here."

"And?"

"And I believe this land is beginning to look like the land you started off in. Have you heard any animals since we found the stream?"

"No." This thought startled Pete because he knew he experienced the same thing earlier.

"You see? The only sound we hear is this stream, which is really more like a river anyways. There is nothing else. I'm figuring out the damned destroy life or take it away or something. Whatever the case, I bet that this same thing is happening to my village."

Amy leads Pete across the path she understands he took. As they are walking, the grayish ground begins to turn into patches of grass. The sparse grass turns in a fuller and fuller grass. Amy notices something else too. In the air, there is a smell she remembers from long ago. She cannot quite place it. Then she notices a different looking thing on the ground. She stops and drops on her knees to look at the thing.

"Why are we stopping?" asks Pete.

"What is this?" wonders Amy.

She picks up the thing that she couldn't place. It has ten little things coming out of the center. The center being a blackish color. She puts her face to it and smells it.

"Pete. What is this? I remember this from when I was a girl."

She puts the item to Pete's nose. Pete laughs, "really? You didn't have flowers in the town where you came from?"

"Oh, that's right. That's what it is called." Amy giggles in delight of finding out.

Amy spends her time over the rest of the trip down the path to visit every flower. Pete knows when she finds one because she squeals in delight, drops his hand or arm, and runs away. This is okay for the first twenty or so times, but eventually Pete is tired of all the stopping, so he speaks.

"Not that flower smelling is bad or anything, but can we get moving? I mean, we still have a way to go, I'm sure. It took me a full day to get to the border of your village. I'm sure the sun, or whatever you guys call it, is about to set."

Pete hears no response and panics. *What if Amy leaves him? He cannot go on his journey alone. He needs someone! He needs her!*

"Amy!" Pete yells.

"Amy!" Pete's voice cracks.

"You would be so hopeless without me," laughs Amy. She is right behind Pete. She cracks up, rolling on the ground and cannot stop laughing.

"Is the big strong man scared to be alone?" Amy continues to laugh.

"Stop laughing! This is not funny!" yells Pete.

"Here." says Amy. "Take a sniff of this. It will make you feel better.

"I don't want to! I just wanna go!"

Amy precedes to shove a bunch of flowers into the face of Pete. Pete gasps for air and takes in the smell of the flower. He coughs and takes a dive towards the ground. Amy laughs all the louder at this predicament. Pete cannot help but realize this moment is funny too and laughs along with her.

After a good solid laugh of an hour or two they are tiring of laughing.

"Pete, I know full well this is hilarious and all, but my stomach is really hurting bad."

"Same, but I cannot stop laughing!"

"It must be these flowers. They must be bewitched!" laughs Amy. "They are probably like those drugged up poppies from Oz. You think someone drugged this flowers for us?" Amy stops for a second as she briefly makes a connection with her former world once again.

Somehow that makes sense to Pete and he wonders, while he's laughing, but he says, "we need to go! Quickly come to me and lead me on. Now!"

Amy comes over to Pete and they continue on their way.

As Amy is leading him, Pete has clearer thoughts. *The voices left them a while ago, but what if they are using a new tactic? What if they are trying to distract them in a different way? Hmm ... it seems to make sense to him.*

Amy seems to be coming to her senses too. She says nothing and her pace quickens. Her tone of voice, for the little bit she speaks (in the next few hours) is much less sweet. She was even getting impatient with him for being too slow.

She is probably going through withdraw! Pete reasons and laughs to himself.

They pass out of the forest and before them is an open field. There is long grass all around and flowers everywhere. There isn't a tree in front of them.

"This looks like a field of grass. There is nothing more before us. Where do we go now?"

"This is where I spoke with the invisible girl. I came to this field after coming out of the dark forest and heard both a boy and girl, but couldn't see them. I don't know where to go. What are we looking for?"

Amy walked for a while and sat down in the field of grass.

Sighing she said, "I'm not really sure. I have never been this far before. Do you remember which way these invisible kids went?"

"Nope, they just disappeared."

"Well, I told you about my father hearing voices. One day he left saying he would follow the voice he heard. He said nothing more than that."

"Did he say anything about the type of voice or where it came from?"

"Not that I remember, he just said he would follow it."

"Well, we can't go back because of those creatures the …"

"Damned."

"Yeah them. And we cannot go back to the dark forest where I met the kids at the edge of it. We must go another way. Is there a north, south, east, west in this world?"

Amy laughed, "you mean directions? Yes, of course there are directions. We have maps, but the village's maps stop at about the forest. We have never gone this far before. This is all new for us. I don't even know much about the dark forest you speak off, but I have heard of it. Besides that, this is a mystery."

"Darn."

Which way do we go? thought Pete. *We cannot go the same way. There is no way we should go back to that dark forest.*

"I wish I could have my sight back. I am tired of not seeing."

"I have an idea."

Before Pete could ask what the idea was, he felt himself falling towards the ground, and there was a horrible pain to the head.

CHAPTER TWENTY-THREE

Pete awoke talking. "Hey! What was that Amy? Did you notice what happened. Something hit me in the head."

Pete heard a rustle and noticed that someone was moving towards him.

"Pete, you okay, man? Your head must really be messed up. Who's Amy?"

It took Pete a few minutes to realize who was speaking to him. "Is this Zach?"

"Yep. Hey, listen Pete, I have been trying to find Tom for a few hours now, and a way out of this house. The house is locked and everything is dark now. I can't see anything outside. There is this fog or mist around the house. Creepy I tell ya; this must be the point before we are killed or something. But, anyways, you need to get up. I can't find Tom anywhere and we need to get out of this house."

Pete was connecting the dots to what was going on. He got up from the couch and started toward where Zach's voice was coming from.

"There's one thing you should know. I cannot see anything."

"Same with me. There seems to be no light coming into this house anymore. That's why I need your help. Do you have candles, a lighter, or matches?"

"Yeah, they're in the kitchen, but Zach, my kitchen is cursed or something. I've had strange smells come from that room. Smells like death and I have seen some floating thing covered in black."

"Well, we can't worry about that right now. Show me where they are."

Pete found Zach by walking into him and grabbed his arm. He pulled the arm to his face, but he couldn't see anything.

"I can't even see your arm when it is right in front of me!"

"Yeah, let's find those candles, and Pete, good news is, if a floating thing covered in black is in the kitchen at least we cannot notice it." Zach laughed.

"Hey, that's pretty funny." Pete stated dryly. "Here take my hand."

"Yes sir! I have been looking forward to the day we could hold hands." Zach says jokingly.

Pete laughed at that, but stated, "shut up boy. In every movie the people always get separated and die one by one."

"True."

Pete leads Zach through the pitch-black living room, to the kitchen, that should be down the hallway on the left. After bumping into everything along the way, they reach the hallway. Pete puts his hand along the left side of the wall, and keeping hold of Zach in his right, he begins to move along the wall.

"Okay, we are getting close to the kitchen, it will be up here on our left."

He continues along the wall until he reaches an opening.

"Here's the kitchen. The candles and matches will be on the far side of the kitchen, to the left of the fridge, in the middle drawer. I will move along the wall with my right hand, so let's switch hands."

"This must be getting serious. I get to hold both your hands in one night." jokingly says Zach.

By this point Pete has had enough and switches hands, finds the right side of the wall, and moves along it. He gets to the right corner of the kitchen.

"Now we just have to go down to the left, along this wall, past the fridge, and we will be set."

He moves his right hand along the cupboards and reaches the end of the corner to the left.

"Alright Zach, I will let go of your hand so I can look through the drawer."

"Fine by me. I'll just put my hand on your shoulder so you know I'm still here."

"Now you're thinking."

Pete went through the clutter of the drawer to search for the candle and matches. He shuffled through a bunch of papers and cards to get to the candles in the back. He pulls them out and puts them on top of the table. After a few more moments he pulls out the matches too. He lights one candle, and the corner of the kitchen lights up.

"There you go Pete! Let me put my arms around your waist and give you a thank you kiss on the cheek." says Zach while suppressing a laugh..

Pete has had enough; after Zach puts his hands on his waist, he grabs the candle and turns around to give him a good kick to the stomach.

Zach begins to laugh as Pete turns around and at first Pete cannot see anything in front of him.

"Hey Zach, where did you go?"

"I'm right here, boy. Right in front of you." Zach laughs, but for the first time Pete is not sure the laugh is coming from Zach anymore.

Pete realizes, to his horror, there is a blackness in front of him. Pete gasped and backs up to the cabinet, bumping into it with his back. He looks down at where the feet of the blackness should be, but nothing is there.

The black floating figure laughs in a horrible voice. Pete wants to run out the kitchen to the left, but he cannot move. The figure moves closer to Pete and continues to laugh.

"I have you Pete. I have you. There's no point in trying anymore. You cannot get away. It's time to give up. It's time to pay back what I gave you. It's time to give me what is mine." The black figure goes for Pete and gives a tug deep inside his chest.

Pete feels faint and collapses to the ground.

As Pete passes out he hears: "Give it to me! Give it to me! It will soon be mine! You cannot fight for him forever! He is not yours!"

CHAPTER TWENTY-FOUR

Startled, Pete wakes up. His head doesn't hurt, but his chest area does and he is gasping for air. Also, he can see, and Amy is now right in his face. She looks worried sick.

"Hey Pete! What's wrong?"

Amy pushes away Pete's hands from his chest and feels his heartbeat. She listens for a few moments and has a perplexed look on her face.

Pete is still gasping for air, and pushing Amy's hand away, he rolls over to his side. Pete wants to speak, but he cannot. He feels his heart, wondering if he is having a heart attack.

To Pete's dismay, his heart seems to function fine.

Amy pulls Pete back over on his back and asks, "Pete, your heart is beating fine. Where does it hurt?"

Pete only motions towards his heart. He tries to speak once again, but he cannot.

At this point Pete is turning blue in the face.

"What the heck Pete! Don't you go dying on me. Once a wimp, always a wimp, but I need your help. I need to find my father, and you need to help!"

Amy pounds on Pete's chest with a small hope that might fix the issue.

At this point, Pete stops breathing, but Amy only hits all the harder. She also yells out loud for help, to no one in particular.

After a few more moments, Amy gives up, backs off of the lifeless body, and falls to her left side, landing on the soft grass. She closes her eyes and tries to think of nothing.

Suddenly, there is a rustle, and Amy hears a couple voices in the distance.

"Did they both die?" says a voice that sounds like a younger boy.

"Oh no! Are we too late?" says a voice that sounds like a younger girl.

"Maybe so."

Amy still has her head on the ground, and her eyes are closed. She hears the two get close to Pete.

"Looks like we might be too late with this one." The boy sighs and drops to the ground.

"Is there anything we can do?" asks the girl.

"Come on. You know this look. He is gone for good. Let's check the other one."

Amy still tries not to move, but at this point she cannot stop shaking.

"Oh, she is alive for sure!" excitedly says the girl.

"Are you okay Amy?" asks the boy.

Even now, Amy cannot move. She tries to open her eyes, but she cannot.

"I think she is in shock." says the boy.

"It's okay Amy, you will be fine. Your friend, unfortunately, is dead. Dead as a doornail, gone from this world. Kaput! Fini…"

The girl cuts him off, "you can stop right there, she doesn't need to hear that."

"Amy, I want you to try to relax, okay? Listen to my voice. I need you to sleep, and you will feel better when you wake up. Don't worry Amy, we will be here to watch you. To protect you, to keep you safe. Sleep, my child. Sleep…"

Amy was still struggling to stop shaking, but was trying to stop. She closed her eyes and fell asleep. She is asleep for what it seems is a long time.

Amy still has her eyes closed, but she hears voices in the background. It is the boy and girl. She tries to hear what they are saying, but she cannot hear very much. The most she comprehends is, "should we tell her?" Strange she would only hear that statement because now she wanted to know more.

Amy rolls over to where the voices are, but sees no one.

"Hey, where are you?"

There is silence for a few moments, and then the boy speaks, "you are going crazy Amy, we are right in front of you. The question should be where are you?"

"What? I'm right here, but where are both of you?"

"We have always been here, from beginning to end."

Amy hears a loud thump and a yell from the boy.

"Hey that was unnecessary!"

"No, it was necessary," states the girl, "you are the one who's crazy and you're only confusing this poor dear."

Amy had to shake her head is disbelief. The boy, acted like a boy, a jerk–a boy really and the girl acted like a caring women.

What was going on?

"Okay, so I'm going to count to ten and both of you are going to appear, then I can breathe easily."

"You are already breathing tho…" The boy began, but another thump was heard.

"Stop that," says the girl. "We are already here, and you are already here. You cannot see us, but we can see you. You are not crazy, but you are in danger, and you need to get away from here. We cannot help you, you are not on your own, but you do not know it yet. We thought for sure your friend would continue to follow the help, but he strayed. Because of his failure to follow he is now gone for good. Let it be a lesson to you, my little one. You must follow the voice of truth."

"But how do I know which voice is that?"

"You can never be sure, but it is a voice that is hard to hear and easy to ignore."

"This doesn't make any sense." Amy says while shaking her head.

"It makes sense, only not to you right now. Your friend made the wrong choice, he is gone because of his choice. There is nothing we can do for him now, but we can help you find the way."

"What is the way?"

"Right."

"You mean this way?" and Amy turns her head to the right to determine.

"No, we mean that the way is right."

Amy is frustrated at this point. "What does that mean anyways? Just tell me what to do."

"You already know what to do, it is what your father did long ago."

"My father disappeared and left me. He said he was hearing voices, and everyone thought he was going crazy. You're saying he was not crazy?"

"My child, your father was crazy, in a sense, but that's what it takes to find the way. You will go through many trials, and it will be quite hard, but I believe you have a chance, unlike your friend."

"You mean there is hope I can make it to where my father is?"

"Yes, but it is more than that."

"So what do I do now?"

"Follow the voice, when it tells you to move, move; when it tells you to stop, stop."

"What if I follow the wrong voice?"

"Then you die like your friend." The boy stated quickly so the girl could not stop him.

The girl sighed, but soon after stated, "he is sadly right, you must follow the voice, or I'm afraid you could be gone too."

"Can you both help me? I'm not sure what to do."

Amy waited for a response, but after a few minutes of asking and waiting, she heard nothing. At this point, Amy sighed and rolled over in the grass to her left.

"Ouch!" Amy screams and quickly rolls over back to her right. Her back hurts immensely and she gets up to examine what she rolled onto. Looking at the location, and because of the tall grass, she cannot make out what happened, so she gets on her knees and works her way through the brush. She comes across a large metal object and after picking it up she notices it is a shield.

This could come in handy, Amy thinks to herself.

Now the shield is covered in dirt, and Amy can tell this is from a different tribe than hers, but the shield is light, and she can tell it is made by a skilled craftsman.

Amy takes a look at her surroundings and finds that there are fields as far as the eye can perceive. She turns every way to see where she came from in regards to the forest. She even looks for Pete, but recognized that he, too, cannot be found.

After looking around for a while, she spots something far in the distance: so far that she cannot tell what it might be.

Amy makes her way towards the something. As time passes on, she notices it is a building of some sort, and she also notes that the sun is a lot lower in the horizon than what Amy was expecting, so she runs.

She glides through the grass in her warrior dress, a summer dress every warrior wears during the heat of the year. Even as Amy is in top shape, being a skilled warrior in her tribe, she realizes she is not becoming tired from running and she is moving quickly.

It is as if the grass is helping her, pushing her along. Amy pushes this thought away because she knows the sun is setting and continues to run with quicker strides.

As Amy makes her way to the building, she runs way around the building to find the door. After looking around the whole building, she cannot find any opening.

This building is simple, made of brick and is a decent size, but Amy wonders if she is imagining the building, so she walks up to it and touches it. It feels cold to the touch, but when she does touch it, something happens. Words appeared.

A story of old would help you here; this building is impenetrable to everything. Walk around this building 7 times then scream, it's possible something might appear.

"Well, that's just stupid," says Amy out loud. "That makes no sense."

Amy takes her hand from the wall and the words disappear. She puts her hand back on the wall, but the words do not come back.

Seeing that the sun has almost set, and she has no other options, she does as the writing on the wall said and walks around the building.

After walking around the building 7 times, she stops and then screams as loud as she can. She keeps on screaming until all the air departs her lungs.

"Yeah that did n..."

Amy stops speaking, because in front of her, a door to the building appears. Amy runs up to the door and tries to open it. It opens with ease, and she steps inside.

Inside, everything is dark and quiet. She searches the side of the wall for a light switch, then realizes that this world does not have electricity. It was at that moment, something else clicked in her. Amy remembered light switches and electricity, but how? And why?

She laughs at herself and turns around to walk out the door, but the door closes. Amy runs to the place where the door once was, but finds it is now just a wall. She is in complete darkness and turns her back once again to the wall and rests her back to it.

"What do I do now? I need light!"

With those words there begins to be a bright glow that comes and fills the room with light. She looks to her left, to where the source of the light is, and finds that the shield she found is glowing brightly. In fact, it is too bright to gaze directly at for long.

The room she is in is not too wide, but quite long. She cannot make out the end. The walls are empty as is the whole room. The floor is a grayish rock color; she touches it and it is cold. At that moment, she realizes there is a cool draft coming from the direction she is facing. Amy moves forward towards the draft.

As she makes her way across the hallway, she looks back to which she came. She cannot see the wall on the side to which she came and, although she had been moving through this hallway for a while, still cannot see anything but moving darkness in front of her.

Amy has the strange sensation she is being watched. The things watching her do not want her here. She looks around in all directions; there is just nothing in the hallway, but still the strange fearful sensation remain. She remembers an old poem that her father used to tell her when she was afraid. It went something like this:

Though I walk through the shadow of the valley of death, I will fear no evil for you are with me.

Amy now wonders who the 'you' is in that poem. She cannot remember, it seems so long ago, like a different lifetime.

She continues to make her way in the hallway, and with each step, which brings her more fear, she stops and mumbles to herself. "I am a Gheon warrior! I have been through worse things than this. I can do this!"

She continues to move once again, but she hears whispers. At first she cannot hear what they say, but they grow louder as time passes on. Soon she can understand the whispers jeering.

"I am a Gheon warrior. Hehe. I have been through worse things than this. I can do this. Hehe."

The voices are mocking her, and soon they are coming from all around her.

She stops once again in fear and looks around.

The shadows are moving! She thinks to herself. *They are real and alive!*

Amy panics and hyperventilate. She cannot keep moving forward, nor is she able to turn around. She is stuck in fear and cannot move, so she falls to the ground on her knees. Something is pushing her down! She looks up. There are shadows coming towards her on the ceiling too! Whatever it is, it is making it hard for her to move and breathe like there is a thousand living things in the room and they are all taking up space.

"Please!" She whispers with her face now on the ground. "I cannot do this alone."

She soon after remembers the conversation she had with the two children and she pleads for their help.

CHAPTER TWENTY-FIVE

Amy awakens in a daze and tries to move her body, but she cannot. With her head also fixed in place, she can only move her eyes. Her legs are sprung high in the air with her head close to the ground, but off it. She is at a 45 degree angle to the ground with her body being straight. Amy moves and tries to cry out, but her lips do not move.

Her body makes its way into a room and she can see an end table with a lamp on top of it. Footsteps are heard from a distance and then two human legs appear in front of her. Amy can only see from the knees down. She hears a voice say to her: "Do not listen to your advisers."

With a startle she awakes on the cold floor. Dazed and trying to remember where she is, she gets up from off the floor. As she stumbles to her feet, she realizes that she can now see everything in this hallway. She looks all around her. In every direction she can make out the floors, the walls, and the ceiling. Amy looks at the ground, finds the shield, and picks it up, but this time she notices an inscription on the back of the shield.

The shield glows in time of need and gives light to shadows. Be wary of the shadows, for you cannot fight them and the shield cannot help you.

Amy puts the shield back on her left arm and moves on to the door at the far end.

After taking a step she stops.

Amy wonders, *the hallway is not that large. I felt like I moved for hours before and never made it to the door, but now the door on the opposite side is only a few feet away. What could make this so?*

Amy then thinks of the strange dream she had. *I feel like the dream was real, but who are my advisers?*

Amy shrugs off the thought and opens the door. The light from the shield fills the room and she notices a table in the middle of the room. She walks to the table and finds a necklace on top. Amy grabs the necklace off the table and feels a warm sensation go through her body. She looks at the charm that is on the necklace, but there is nothing special about it. It is just a standard necklace and she puts the necklace around her neck.

At once, in front of Amy appears a door. She goes to the door that is standing right in the middle of the room and looks at both sides. There is a door handle on either side, and Amy wonders which end she is suppose to go through. As she is contemplating, her neck begins to burn. She grabs for the necklace, but finds it is not around her neck, it has burned its way into her skin.

Amy now in extreme pain, is on the ground and screaming. She tries to get the necklace off of her.

At once the pain stops and she grabs for the necklace around her neck, but still cannot find it.

Amy sighs and gets up from the ground. The doorway with two entrances is still right in front of her.

She opens one of the doorways and steps inside.

Her body is twisted and warped as she enters. She feels a quick cooling sensation and she recognizes she is being moved into a different world. This world differs from her own, and she is not sure what the different buildings that are forming in front of her are, but soon, the buildings disappear.

She looks at the ground she is on and realizes it is firm. She cannot remember ever stepping on this before. Amy notices that the color of the ground is black, and that the smell coming from it differs from she has ever experienced. She looks about herself and finds she is in the middle of a long stretch of a black surface with yellow line marks.

Amy, bending at her knees, reaches down and touches the ground. She is in awe, and has a shocking expression on her face, as she looks from the ground to the surrounding area.

She steps to the other side of the black surface and stops in front of a sign. The sign has a drawing on it, and as she continues to stare at it, she begins to remember she use to know what the drawings meant.

What was this called? This must be a type of way for people to write down what they spoke. Like what her tribe would do. Although, the words are all strange and don't look like anything she has ever seen before.

Turning to the left and right, looking past the sign, Amy sees only a long stretch of nothing. On either side of the black path are trees which slope down from the path.

Amy turns around and heads towards the middle of the black path and turns right, when, there is a loud noise to her left, and then silence.

CHAPTER TWENTY-SIX

Amy wakes up in a gasp and finds she is on the floor. Straight behind her is the door frame, and she tries to reach for it, but finds she cannot move. Her head and her body will not respond to what she is thinking. She panics and realizes that she cannot feel anything, from her head down, but the pain in her head is unbearable.

There are voices all around her. They are whispering terrible things inside her head, telling her things like, *it's over, just give up, there is nothing you can do, look how you failed.* She sees a darkness begin to fill the room, but the voices and the darkness disappear.

After a few moments, Amy notices she is not the only person in the room. In front of her she sees a white light moving back and forth. She cannot tell what this is, except that the light is bright and it cannot be looked at.

The bright light moves towards her and flies past.

At that moment, the door to her back opens and Amy hears shrieking; the outer door to the place opens, and soon after there is silence.

The silence is painful, but Amy hears a pair of soft footsteps. The steps are running towards her, and she can understand words coming from them. It is the voice of the kids.

"Get up Amy! Get out, you are not safe here! Quickly!"

Amy gets up, without realizing it, grabs the shield, turns around, and heads straight through the door frame, and then through the door to the room. She stops for a few seconds at the entrance to the hallway, but taking a deep breath, she runs as fast as she can through the hallway to the open door at the end.

She reaches the door and rushes through. Enjoying the bright light on her skin and the fresh breeze, she runs a short distance from the building and collapses onto the grass.

"What just happened?" she asked herself.

She looks herself over and she seems to be okay.

Amy takes a few minutes to recuperate and falls asleep.

When she wakes up, the sun is shining bright and she hears birds around her. I must be okay! Perhaps this was all just a dream!

Amy gets up and looks around. Disappointed, she spots the building she ran from yesterday, and puts her head down on her hands as she begins to weep. She hasn't cried for ages, a Gheon warrior doesn't cry, but since she believes she is alone, she doesn't care.

Once Amy is done sobbing, she still is not sure what to do. She looks all around her. There is the building in front of her, but nothing else. As far as the eye can perceive, there are trees, grass, and some very distant hills.

Amy walks up to the building and looks for a door. Not finding one, she touches the same area she touched yesterday, but nothing appears. She runs around the building 7 times and yells like before, but a door doesn't appear.

Amy realizes that she needs to get back to that land she was in for a short time yesterday, but there seems to be no way back the way she came.

She turns around again and rests her back on the wall looking out from the building. She looks and waits for something to happen. Then she remembers!

"The kids will know what to do!" she says aloud.

Amy calls out for them, but after a while she gives up as no response is received.

She realizes she is hungry, so she walks away from the building and heads towards one tree. As she makes her way through the tall grass, she looks about herself to make sure someone is not following her and to determine where she is. As she is looking about, she is aware of a strong tug on her left hand.

The shield falls from her hand and she trips over it. Landing with the left side of her face hitting the ground first. Even as she is in a daze, a rush of excitement stores up in her.

There in front of her is the shield. She grabs it and instinctively studies the back of it. The words from yesterday are gone and new words are in its place.

Yup ... it's over.

"Now what does that mean?" Amy asks aloud.

She looks again at the shield and new words have formed once again.

Just playing bro.

Bro? What's a bro? And did this shield really answer her? she wonders.

Amy looks back at the shield in haste, but the words have not changed. She laughs to herself and says what she thought a moment before.

A bro is a friend of the male companionship. Yes.

"But, I'm a female!" exclaimed Amy.

Okay, chick.

"What's a chick?"

The young of a chicken or a slang term for a female.

Frustrated, Amy throws the shield as far as she can from her.

"You happy now! I threw you!" Amy yells, while getting up from the ground. She walks over to shield and picks it up.

Ouch.

Amy laughs and falls to the ground once more, she continues to laugh until she cannot anymore. She pulls the shield to her side again and looks at what is written, but nothing appears.

"What is your name?"

What is a name, but a way to address someone? You may call me what you would like.

"What are you?"

A shield.

"When did you come about?"

I do not know.

"What are you used for?"

Blocking things.

Amy laughed again. It's almost like this shield has a personality.

"What am I supposed to do now?"

I do not know.

"What are you good at?"

Blocking things, if the person using me is good at it.

"That's an old joke."

No, that's the truth.

"What about glowing? You glow."

Do I? I cannot see so I cannot be sure. Thanks for letting me know. ;)

"What is that at the end of your words?"

A wink.

"What is a wink?"

Quickly closing one eye.

"Why would you wink at me?"

I was flirting.

"Wha...", but before Amy could ask a response appeared.

Social interaction between two people to show interest in the person. Flirting shows "liking."

"How can you like me, I am a female, and you are a shield?"

Why would I not like you? I have no one else to write to.

"When is the last time you talked to someone?"

You are the first.

"Are you lonely?"

I am a shield.

"Is there anything you can do to help me?"

What do you need help with?

"I'm not sure what to do now."

Tell me what has happened.

Amy spent the rest of the day going over everything that had happened. She talked about her old tribe and growing up there, she talked about the damned, and how she had to flee her village, she spoke about Pete and him dying. Amy continued on with the children, the building with the passageway (which led to a room), the necklace, the room, the door in the middle of the room, and the other world. She spoke about the way she awoke and came back and ran out of the room. Anything that came to Amy's mind, she spoke about.

After she was finished, she paused and waited for the shield to respond. The shield did not respond, so she asked it, "What do you think?"

I have confirmed you are a female.

"Come on shield!" She bashed the shield on the ground multiple times. "No, I mean about the story?"

Was the story a question?

"No, but what should I do now?"

I am a shield. I am used to defend.

"So you are saying you cannot help?"

What do you need help with?

"You are annoying! You are probably the most frustrating thing I have ever talked to!" Amy was mad and yelling now.

I am a shield. Have you ever talked to a shield before?

"No."

Then how would you know what to expect?

Amy sighed and pulled her head back and looked up at the sky. It was soon after she noticed that it was pitched black out. She looked back at the shield and it was glowing bright.

"Shield, why do you glow?"

Yes, yes! I forgot to tell you, I can glow too! A double use ... no ... triple use shield!

"So why?"

Don't be afraid ... well, then again, perhaps you should .... I only glow when the shadows are out.

"You mean nighttime?"

I do not glow at night, only when shadows are close by. Do you see any shadows?

"I cannot tell, there is darkness all around me, I cannot see anything."

Is it nighttime?

"I suppose so, but I cannot see stars, everything is black."

I am afraid to say ... what was your name?

"Amy."

Amy, the shadows are all around you now. You cannot see anything because the shadows block you from seeing anything they want you to see. I have realized my purpose now. You must visualize where you were facing and head towards the building you spoke of. Hold on tight to me!

"Will the door be there now?"

I do not know, all I understand is that these shadows suck life by feeding on life itself and feeding on fear.

"I think I have the right way. Can these shadows hurt you?"

I am a shield, but they can hurt you, as you have already mentioned.

Amy makes her way, with heavy movement, across the grass, only being able to perceive a foot around the glowing shield. It was in this moment that Amy realizes that everything is silent. She cannot make out anything about her except the sound of the grass brushing along her. It is almost as if the sound is stopped by the shadows. As well as the sound being stopped, it is almost as if the surrounding sound is louder, like it is being reflected.

She continues to walk, but realizes that she has walked more than she should have. She should have made it back to the building.

"I can help you!" A voice cries out in the darkness. As Amy follows the voice, she looks at the writing on the shield.

I wouldn't listen. It is worse than I thought! The shadows seem to speak!

Amy doubles back, but even though she did not stray far, the damage has been done. She doesn't quite remember which way she was going.

Amy, not realizing that the shadows can understand her, talks out loud to the shield.

"I'm not sure where I should go!" Panic is in her voice. "I have lost my way!"

Do not be afraid, for I am with you.

It was from the poem that her father told her as a child! Amy thought.

It's not just a poem.

Amy froze, the shield said it couldn't hear her thoughts, but could it? Was she being lied to this whole time? Maybe she should have not listened to it.

Why would I lie to you? I am a shield. I gave you what you needed to know at the time. Nothing more.

"So you know what I need to do now?"

I am a shield.

Amy walked again, her breathing was heavy, and she felt stuffy, almost like she couldn't get enough oxygen.

I can hear you breathe that is not good. You need to relax.

But Amy could not relax. She panicked and wondered why she hasn't seen anyone from her village. Were they all gone now? What was she suppose to do now? She could see nothing and only had a shield to help her. How would that help her?

Thoughts continued to flood into Amy, thoughts she could not control. The darkness seemed to be all around her.

She looked again at the shield.

Everything will be okay.

Except she didn't understand how that would be possible.

"Death is upon her now!"

"She cannot make it."

"Trouble breathing are we?"

"Just give up."

Amy listened to these voices and many others; they were now flooding her mind. She looked one last time to read the words of the shield, but passed out before comprehending them.

"You are gone," was the last voice she comprehends.

CHAPTER TWENTY-SEVEN

Amy awoke in a startle. She was breathing heavily, and the left side of her body was in extreme pain. There was a bright light above her, and she tried to look about. Amy became aware of a lady's voice from behind her and felt the lady push her down. Amy tried to speak but something was in her mouth, and it was coming out of her mouth too, and was connected to something that was to her left.

"Doctor, she woke! Doctor, doctor, get back here!"

The doctor walked back into the room, having just left.

"Whoa Caroline, the anesthesiologist put her out just an hour ago. Get him on the phone now."

"Yes, sir."

The lady that held Amy down walked away, and the doctor walked up to Amy and spoke.

"Everything will be okay, don't struggle. Just rest."

"Caroline, I need the nursing team back here now!"

"Yes, sir." That lady was farther away now as she was barely understood.

Amy pointed to her chest area, trying to get this person to understand she couldn't breathe. The man seemed to understand, but Amy passed out again.

When she awoke, she could not make out the place she was. Everything was a whitish tan color, but after a few moments, Amy's vision appeared once again. In front of her there was a white wall and a white ceiling. She thought it was unusual that everything looked clean, there was no sign of a mess or sign of how the walls or ceiling were created. They seemed to be covered, and to Amy, fake. She glanced over to her left and saw a door. The first thing that reminded her of the door was that it looked like the doors from the place she came from.

She saw a small table on her left that had a few items Amy couldn't place.

At once, the sunlight was gleaming through the open window to the right and Amy stared and observed how pretty the reflection was on the wall. She continued to watch as the shadows of clouds made their way across the sun's path and then realized her predicament.

Her mouth was clear of the thing from before, but now there was another thing around her nose. She touched it and pulled it out, but after a few moments, put it back into place, as it seemed to help her to breathe.

Amy reached across her body with her right arm, which was bruised, and touched her left arm, or tried to touch it, as it was covered in a white hard kind of casing. She knocked on it, and nothing happened. Amy knocked again on it and asked it a question, hoping it would answer, but again, nothing happened.

Dazed and confused, Amy tried to get up hoping to see what was happening, but her body only moved a little and she rolled back to her original spot on the bed.

Even as it had to be only a few minutes from when she awoke, she was bored and tried to talk, but nothing would come out. It was at that moment she realized she did not speak to the white object on her arm, but only thought what she wanted to speak. It was all in her head. She could only make noises, but couldn't form words together.

Hoping for a bell, she looked around her room to see if there was any way to get a hold of anyone. Still there was nothing, just a white room, with one bed, one small table, one door, and some strange looking things to her right, one of which was connected to her nose.

So Amy waited, for what felt like hours, for someone to come into the room, but no one came.

The light, which was illuminating across the wall in front of her, was now gone, and it became a dark orange color.

Silence was all around her, and it was the first time in many years that Amy heard no sound.

She looked at her right arm and pulled off the white strip of sticky material and noticed there was something protruding. As she pulled at it, a burning sensation shot through her right arm, and she stopped for a second.

Quickly she pulled it out and examined it. It was a long pointy thing and had a small hole at the end of it. The other end was connected to a long tube shaped thing and was connected to a clear bag at the end. The bag had nothing in it and had strange markings on it, similar to the ones she found when she first came into this world.

Blood came out of the spot where she took it out of her arm. She grabbed her arm, and noticed it was sore.

Amy pulled off the thing on her nose and swung her legs over the side of the bed to the left. She sighed and got up.

Standing on her two legs, she walked towards the door. She was shaking and stumbled against the wall next to the door. This was the first time she realized she was weak and tired.

Amy fell into the door, put her hand on the knob, and turned it. She tilted back a little, and the door swung open.

With the door opened, Amy took a deep breath and stepped through.

Everything around her was bright, and she fell down shielding her eyes. Amy put her face to the ground and noticed something tickled.

It was grass, but even the grass was bright. Her eyes hurt, and couldn't stand the brightness, but the light was beautiful. Amy could not stop from keeping her eyes open. She shielded her eyes with one hand, staring into the glimpses of light.

Out in the silence, Amy heard a voice, a gentle and soft, powerful, but caring voice called to her.

"Rise up my child and follow me."

Amy got up as the voice commanded her. She asked the voice, "can I stop shielding my eyes?"

"I'm afraid you cannot my child because we do not want you to see, but only listen. Listen to the words I tell you. Your Father is here, waiting for you. But, it is not your time yet, we want you back in the other worlds. Just remember that it is not because we need you, but because we want you. You are not special, you are chosen by us."

Amy strained to understand what this voice was telling her, but nothing came to her mind, except that this must be god, she was in Imdagos, and she was bowing down to him whether she wanted to or not.

"What do I do?" Amy cried out.

Hearing nothing she repeated once again. "What do I do?"

As everything in the bright world faded, she found everything was dark, but she was still talking, repeating, "what do I do?"

Her words remained soft and seemed like they were distant.

In a flash, her eyes opened to darkness. She tried to look around, but there was no light around her.

It was not the darkness that bothered her, but the sounds. From all around her, she could pick up screaming. The voices continued with each distinguishable from one another, male and female, and they remained in pain. Amy hated the sounds and this place; she would do anything to get away. There were strange emotions running through her: pain, hate, fear, sadness, but the strongest one was the loneliness.

For the first time in a long time, Amy desired to be with people. With anyone, it didn't matter who. She felt empty and lost.

Amy tried to cry out to the surrounding voices, but she could not … and then silence.

CHAPTER TWENTY-EIGHT

Someone was lightly shaking her, and she awoke to the soft whispering of someone to her left.

As she opened her eyes, she looked over and noticed someone was talking to her. For a split second, she cried out in fear, but the face was kind, caring, and concerned.

"How are you feeling?" the lady asked.

Amy looked around the room. It was the same room she was in before: the one she was dreaming. Or was it a dream?

Maybe, which was a dream was a better question, she wondered.

"Ener eq gerdododt."

The lady, looked at her puzzled? "I'm sorry, can you say that again?"

"Ener eq gerdododt." Amy said slowly, not sure why the nurse was puzzled.

"Do you speak English? I'm sorry, I don't speak what you do."

Amy nodded, but was confused.

"You are speaking gibberish, Ms. I cannot understand you."

Amy, pointed at her hand, and moved it along, forming words, looking at the lady in between.

The lady seemed to understand and left the room. Moments later she came back with two items, one was thin white pieces of something, and the other was some type of tool.

The lady handed the items to Amy, but Amy just stared at it. Understanding her confusion, the lady took the items back, and showed how these two strange tools where to be used. One was for writing the characters down, and the other was to write the characters upon.

After Amy was given the two tools, she wrote what she said before. *Ener eq gerdododt,* and handed the tool used for writing characters to the lady.

"I'm sorry, I do not understand your language."

Amy was frustrated and couldn't understand what she was hearing. This lady was speaking perfect Phorgine!

She swung her legs over to the left, and got up not realizing that she still had the thing in her nose, and her right arm was still connected to the clear bag.

"No, please, stop! I cannot allow you to leave: you are still recovering. Please lie back down ...

security … security!" The lady was yelling and in a panic.

As Amy noticed she was still connected, she pulled both objects which obscured her, and took off past the nurse. She made her way to the already open door, hesitated for a split second, and ran through.

She makes a right and heads down the hallway.

Outside of her room she realizes that all the walls here are in white. There are doors to her right and to her left. She makes her way to the place with two doors and without thinking, pushes through them. With doors causing her issues, she stops and realizes she went through another door. Also, she notices the strange lights right above her. One of them is flickering with an unnatural glow.

At once, Amy sees a couple people in front of her. They seem to think her important and began to chase her.

She doubles back through the double door and, not realizing how hallways and rooms work in this world, makes a quick left into the open door to her left.

Finding a room similar to when she first awoke in this world, she sees someone on the bed like he is asleep. Walking up to this person, she sees it is someone familiar. Except for his face, he has a white blanket covering him, and strange things connected to him.

She leans in to inspect, and realizes he has a similar thing in his mouth, and also a similar thing in his nose.

Even though she realizes this is Pete, she is emotionless and backs away because of the current situation.

She runs out of the room and proceeds to the left. The people who chased her, once far away, are now just coming through the double doors behind her. She runs past her room, and through another set of double doors. As she's running through this new area, she hears voices. As she is coming closer to the voices, she realizes there is a bunch of people cluttered in a room.

A few of them look up at her, but most of them are not interested in the commotion. Amy reasons, *maybe it's that whatever is in their hands is more interesting.* Looking over to her right, she sees a women around a wooden object.

This lady looks up at her and speaks. "Are you okay?"

Amy ignores this person and continues on past the crowd of people. She is just about ready to go through the exit, but realizes there are people coming in from outside. She turns away from them and continues on her way. Amy makes her way through a second double door on the far side of the room from where she entered.

I really need to get away, she thinks. She instinctively knows she can't be captured by these people.

She rushes through the doors and continues to look for another way out of this place. As she proceeds along, she keeps looking over to her left, hoping to find another door out. As she continues along, past many doors, she sees a place to exit.

Coming to a exit, Amy opens it, and walks through feeling very relieved.

Almost outside the door, Amy notices that grass is everywhere, and she continues through it and runs. She hopes that no one has seen her go through this door.

Looking behind, she gasps at the sight of the same building she has been in multiple times. The same stone building she first found and marched around. The same building where this mess became more of a mess.

Turning around she walks up to the stone building and realizes there is no door.

Relieved that she is not being chased anymore, but still quite confused, Amy ponders why she is back in this world. It's the world she knows, but she was hoping she would get answers, especially in regards to seeing Pete.

She also wonders if there's a connection through walking through doors and appearing in new areas. In this area, this world, this place where she lives, there are no doors. In her world, if there is a "door," it's just a sheet or something covering it. Everything is open, everything except this building she is looking at; this building made with stone. In this building is where she found the necklace and met the shadows. It is the same building where she remembered electricity.

As has been common for this journey of Amy's, she has felt lost and confused, and not sure at all what to do.

Thinking longer, she wonders if this is perhaps a good thing. Perhaps she needs to find another door; she can then reach the other world and get answers. Maybe this is how she finds her dad. Maybe this is how she finds her Father.

As Amy turns away from the stone building, she walks around the whole exterior hoping for some answers. All she wants is to find another door.

Not finding one around the building, she continues to walking on past it, and proceeding further than she has ever gone before. As she does so, she continues to ponder many things.

The sun, which was setting to her back, sets off a soft glow on her arms. The light looked beautiful to Amy as it extended past her. It seemed warm and it felt good.

The pleasant sensation dissipates, and Amy felt lost, confused and lonely, but first and foremost, unsure of what to do.

Amy, continuing on her way, reaches an area of the grass field, and finds a tree in the middle of the plain. The sun looking down on the tree causes it to almost glimmer. It is shining from the sun beating down on it: the radiant beauty came from the orange crescent light.

Amy walks up to the tree and realizes it's not just the leaves and the trunk that are glimmering, but there's also something else in the distance leaning against the tree on the ground. It is shimmering in light. It's her shield.

You cannot imagine the joy she felt when, yet again, she realizes she is not alone. There is someone with her, always with her. As Amy continues to walk up to the shield, she sees its beauty contrast the sun's light. Unlike the light Amy was accustomed to see radiating from the shield, this was a brilliant white light. This light gives her peace, hope, encouragement that maybe, just maybe, everything will be okay.

About the Author

Paul Brandt lives in Louisville, KY where he is pursuing a Master's degree at The Southern Baptist Theological Seminary. He works overnight to achieve his dreams and sleeps, at random times. When he is not writing, he enjoys long walks (please no date requests), eating (sometimes), reading, music composition, biking, and laughing. Jesus is important to him too.

Thank you for reading!

Dear Reader,

I hope you enjoyed "Encountering Darkness." While this book has been long in the making, I am thankful I could finish it. Although I am now crafting the next book, and there is a rough draft for the overarching series story, I am open for feedback on this book or thoughts on future books. If you are interested in reaching me for comments, or if you would like to be added to an email list for future books, you can reach me at bookwritergeek@gmail.com.

As you probably notice, reviews can be difficult to come by. You, the reader, have the power to make or break a book. Whether you enjoyed the book, or not, I would love a review of "Encountering Darkness."

In gratitude,

Paul Brandt

Printed in Great Britain
by Amazon